"Thee doesn't belie

Matthew was about to say he didn't, and then he recalled all he'd witnessed today. "I haven't for a long time," he said finally. "Is it a miracle or coincidence that my cousin was one of the men you nursed at Gettysburg?"

"I call it providence," Verity answered.

"Providence?" Matt asked.

"Yes. God knew that I would come here to Fiddler's Grove to open this school for freed slaves."

Matt wished Verity wouldn't wear such a deep-brimmed bonnet. He wanted to watch her vivid expressions. For a woman who radiated peace, she felt and showed everything vibrantly.

As she continued to speak of the providence that brought them to this place, her voice grew stronger with the passion that he loved in her. And hated. *Don't care so much, Verity. That's the way to pain.* He wanted so much more for her.

Books by Lyn Cote

Love Inspired Historical

Her Captain's Heart

Love Inspired

Never Alone
New Man in Town
Hope's Garden
*Finally Home
*Finally Found
The Preacher's Daughter
**His Saving Grace
**Testing His Patience
**Loving Constance
Blessed Bouquets
  "Wed by a Prayer"

*Bountiful Blessings
**Sisters of the Heart

Love Inspired Suspense

†Dangerous Season
†Dangerous Game
†Dangerous Secrets

†Harbor Intrigue

LYN COTE

Lyn Cote married her real-life hero and was blessed with a son and daughter. She loves game shows, knitting, cooking and eating! She and her husband live on a beautiful lake in the north woods of Wisconsin. Now that the children have moved out, she indulges three cats: V-8 (for the engine not the juice), Sadie and Tricksey. In the summer, she writes using her laptop on her porch overlooking the lake. And in the winter she sits by the fireplace her husband installed with the help of a good neighbor during their first winter at the lake. Lyn loves to hear from readers, so visit her Web site at www.LynCote.net, or e-mail her at l.cote@juno.com.

LYN COTE

Her Captain's Heart

Steeple Hill®

Published by Steeple Hill Books™

STEEPLE HILL BOOKS

Steeple
Hill®

Recycling programs
for this product may
not exist in your area.

ISBN-13: 978-0-373-82801-2
ISBN-10:   0-373-82801-2

HER CAPTAIN'S HEART

www.SteepleHill.com

Printed in U.S.A.

Blessed are the peacemakers for they shall
be called the children of God.
—*Matthew* 5:9

I can do all things through Christ
which strengthen me.
—*Philippians* 4:13

Dedicated to my Sunday school teachers, the women and men who first taught me about God, His Son and His Spirit. Florence Brauck, Ruth Silovich, Beatrice Sladek née Nilsen, Gordon Zoehler and others whom only God recalls.

Chapter One

Gettysburg, Pennsylvania, September 1866

Verity Hardy loathed the man, God forgive her. She stood looking down at her late husband's cousin, she on the top step of her wide porch, he on the bottom. The unusually hot autumn sun burned just beyond the scant shade of the roof. Her black mourning dress soaked up the heat that buffeted her in waves, suffocating and singeing her skin. The man had been haranguing her for nearly a quarter of an hour and she didn't know how much more she could take.

"I can't believe you're going through with this insane plan." Urriah Hardy wiped sweat from his brow with the back of his hand and glared at her, his jowly face reddening. He held the reins of his handsome gelding, fidgeting just behind him.

Pressing a hankie to her upper lip, she looked past him to the golden fields beyond. Memories of wounded soldiers—their agonized screams and soul-deep moans—shuddered through Verity. She'd never forget those bloody July days three years ago. She couldn't let them count for naught. Still, her deep uncertainty made her hands tremble. She clasped them together so he wouldn't see this sign of weakness. "Thee knows," she said in a final attempt at politeness, "I've packed everything, and we leave at dawn."

"You're a fool, woman. That renter you've found won't make a go of it. He lost his own farm."

Yes, because he was drafted into the Union Army and thy younger brother, the banker, wouldn't give him more time to pay the mortgage. "That's really none of thy business," she murmured, adding a warning note to her tone.

"You should have rented to me. I'm family."

His reference to family stung her like rock salt. Urriah had cheated on every business deal she'd ever known him to make. "So thee could have cheated me instead?"

After the brazen words popped out of her mouth, conscience stung Verity instantly. *Judge not, lest ye be judged.* But she couldn't—wouldn't—take back the words. She stood her ground, her face hot and set.

He swore at her, vulgar and profane, something no man had ever done in her presence.

Her frayed temper ripped open. "I don't expect thee to understand," she shot back with a disdain she couldn't hide. "Not a coward who bought his way out of the draft."

For a moment he rocked on his toes and she thought he might climb the steps to strike her. Instead, an evil, gloating leer engulfed his ugly face. "Well, since you won't listen to reason, I guess you'll just have to take what comes, down in Dixie. You'll be lucky if the Rebs just run you out of town on a rail. If they lynch you, I'll inherit the land and you know it." He chuckled in a mean way and turned his back to her. "The day a woman bests me will be the day hell freezes over," he taunted as he mounted his horse.

His parting shot drew her down the steps and into the dusty lane. "I've made out a will and thee's not the beneficiary!" she called after him. "Roger's father inherits the land as guardian of Beth."

"I'm a patient man, Quaker." He pulled up the reins, stopping his horse. "I can wait till Roger's father dies and then the court will name me, your daughter's next of kin, guardian of her assets." He doffed his hat in an insolent way and cantered off.

Stiff with disapproval, she watched until she could see only the dust his horse's hooves kicked up in the distance. The hot anger drained out of her, leaving her hollow with regret and worry.

Letting anger rule the tongue was never wise. But

his cutting words had prompted her own doubts. Was she up to the task she'd taken for herself?

Out of the blue, a memory—vivid and as fresh as today—caught her by surprise. Five years earlier, she'd stood in this very spot as her husband had left for war. She could see the back of his blue Union uniform as he marched away from her.

Then he halted in midstride and ran back to her. Pulling her into his arms, he'd crushed her against the rough wool of his jacket. His kiss had been passionate, searching, as if drinking in the very essence of her. "I'll come back to you," he'd promised. "I will."

But he hadn't. Thousands upon thousands had broken that same promise. She'd watched many soldiers die, both gray and blue. And many had keepsakes from wives or sweethearts in their pockets. It broke her heart to think of it.

She wrapped her arms around her. In spite of the scorching sun, the loneliness she'd lived with for the past five years whistled through her like an icy winter wind. "Now I'm leaving, too, dearest one," she whispered.

She'd asked God's blessing on her plans but how had she behaved the day before she left? Shame over her unruly tongue deepened. She covered her face with her hands as if she could hide her hot tears from God.

"I'm sorry, Father, for my temper. I shouldn't have spoken to Urriah like that. But he's…it's such an injustice. He lives and prospers while Roger lies some-where in an unmarked grave in Virginia." She pressed her hands tighter against her face as if pushing back the tears and her unChristian words, feeling as if she couldn't get anything right today.

"Again I must apologize, Father. It is not my job to decide who is worthy of life and who deserves to die." Lowering her hands, she turned back to the house. Her father-in-law and her daughter would be back from their last-minute trip to town anytime now and she had to get a cold supper ready for them.

At the top step, she paused and leaned against the post. "God, I've felt Thy spirit moving within me, Thy inner light. I'm sorry I'm such a weak vessel. Please use me. Let me reflect Thy light in the present darkness."

Fiddlers Grove, Virginia, October

In one routine motion, Matt rolled from the bed, grabbed his rifle and was on his feet. In the moonlight he crouched beside the bed, listening. What had roused him from sleep? He heard the muffled nicker of a horse and a man's voice. Then came knocking on the door. Bent over, Matt scuttled toward the door, wary of casting a shadow.

Staying low, he moved into the hall and ducked into an empty room. He eased over to the uncurtained win-dows overlooking the front porch. From the corner of the window sash, he glanced down. A buckboard stood at the base of the porch steps. A man wearing a sad-looking hat was standing beside it and a little girl sat on the buckboard seat.

"Verity, maybe there is a key under the mat," the man said quietly to a woman hidden under the front porch roof below Matt's window.

Verity? A key? A woman was knocking at his door and looking for a key? And they had a child with them.

"But, Joseph," came her reply from out of sight, barely above a whisper. "This might not be the Barnesworth house. I don't want to walk into some stranger's home uninvited."

She spoke with a Northern accent. And this was or had been the Barnesworth house. Wondering if this was some sort of diversion, he listened for other telltale sounds. But he heard nothing more.

He rose slowly and walked back to his room. He pulled his britches over his long johns and picked up his rifle again. Just because they looked like innocent travelers who had turned up after dark didn't mean that they actually were innocent travelers. Caution kept a man alive.

He moved silently down the stairs to the front hall. Through the glass in the door, he glimpsed a shadowy figure, dressed in a dark color, facing away. He turned the key in the lock, twisted the knob and yanked the door open. "Who are you?" he demanded.

The woman jerked as if he'd poked her with a stick, but did not call out. She turned toward him, her hand to her throat.

"What do you want?" he asked, his rifle held at the ready.

Her face was concealed by shadow and a wide-brimmed bonnet and her voice seemed strangely disembodied when she spoke. "Thee surprised me, friend."

Thee? Friend? "What's a Quaker doing at my door at this time of night?" he snapped.

"No need to take that tone with her," the older man said, moving toward the steps. "We know it's late, but we got turned around. Then we didn't find anywhere to stop for the night and the full moon made travel easy. So we pressed on."

"Is this the Barnesworth house?" the woman asked.

"It was," Matt allowed. "Who are you?"

"I am Verity Hardy. I'm a schoolteacher with the Freedman's Bureau. Who are thee?"

He rubbed his eyes, hoping she would disappear and he'd wake up in bed, wondering why he was having such an odd dream. "Why have you come here?"

"Why, to teach school, of course." Her voice told him that she was wondering if he were still half-asleep. Or worse.

Not a dream, then. His gut twisted. Something had gone wrong. But he forced himself not to show any reaction. The war had taught him to keep his cards close to his chest. He rubbed his chin. "Ma'am, I am—" he paused to stop himself from saying Captain "—Matthew Ritter." But he couldn't keep from giving her a stiff military bow. "I am employed by the Freedman's Bureau, too. Did you come with a message for me? Or are you on your way to some other—"

"This is the Barnesworth house?" the woman interrupted.

He didn't appreciate being cut off. "This was the Barnesworth house. It belongs to the Freedman's Bureau now."

Something moved in the shadows behind the strangers. Matt gripped his rifle and raised it just a bit. He searched the shadows for any other telltale movement. It could just be an opossum or a raccoon. Or someone else with a rifle and lethal intent.

The woman turned her head as if she had noticed his distraction. "Is there anything wrong?"

The older gentleman said, "I think we need to shed some light on the situation." He lifted a little girl with long dark braids from the buckboard and drew her up the steps. "I'm Joseph Hardy. Call me Joseph, as Verity does." He offered Matt his hand. "I'm Verity's father-in-law. Why don't you invite us in, light a lamp and we can talk this out?"

Matt hesitated. If someone else were watching them, it would be better to get them all inside. And he couldn't see any reason not to take them at face value.

Four years of war had whittled down a good deal of his society manners. "Sorry. Didn't mean to be rude."

Matt gripped the man's gnarled hand briefly and then gave way, leading them to the parlor off the entry hall. He lit an oil lamp on the mantel and set the glass globe around the golden point of light. Then he set a vase in front of it, making sure the light was diffused and didn't make them easy targets. He knew what Fiddlers Grove was capable of doing to those with unpopular views.

Turning, he watched the woman sit down on the sofa. She coaxed the little girl, also dressed in black, to sit beside her. Joseph chose a comfortable rocker nearby. Matt sat down on the love seat opposite them, giving him the best view of the front parlor windows. He rested the rifle on his lap at the ready. Now that he had more light, he saw that they looked weary and travel-worn. But what was he supposed to do with them?

He was still unable to make out the woman's face, hidden by the brim of her plain black bonnet. He glanced at her hands folded in front of her. Under her thin gloves he saw the outline of a wedding band on her right hand. Another widow, then. Every town was crowded with widows in mourning. He knew they deserved his sympathy, but he was tired of sidestepping the lures cast toward him.

He watched the woman untie and remove her bonnet. The black clothing, Quaker speech and the title of teacher had misled him. He'd expected mousy brown hair and a plain, older face. But she looked to be around his age, in her midtwenties. Vivid copper-colored hair curled around her face, refusing to stay pulled back in a severe bun. Her almost transparent skin was illuminated by large caramel-brown eyes. The look in those eyes said that, in spite of her fatigue, this widow was not a woman to dismiss. A vague feeling of disquiet wiggled through him.

Why are you here? And how can I get you to leave? Soon?

As if she'd heard his unspoken questions, she began explaining. "I was told in a letter from the Freedman's Bureau to come to this house this week and get settled before I start my teaching duties next week. But I was not told a gentleman would be at this house also." The cool tone of her voice told him that she would not be casting any lures in his direction. In fact, he'd been right. She sounded as disgruntled to find him here as he felt in confronting her.

Good. But what had happened? Matt frowned as he added up the facts. He should have expected something like this—everything had been running too smoothly. The Freedman's Bureau was part of the War Department. And after serving four years in the Union Army, he didn't trust the War Department to get anything right. "There's been a mistake."

"Obviously," Joseph said dryly.

"Would thee mind telling us what thee is here for?" Mrs. Hardy asked him.

He did mind, but he thought an explanation might help resolve the problem. "In general, I'm here to help former slaves adjust to freedom in any way that I can. Specifically, I am here to form a chapter of the Union League of America and to prepare the former slaves to vote. I expect the amendment that will give them that right will be passed in Congress soon. And I'm to get a school built."

Mrs. Hardy quivered as if somebody had just struck her. "The school isn't built yet?"

"Did they tell you it was?" Matt asked, already guessing the answer. His gaze lingered on those caramel eyes that studied him, weighing his words.

Suddenly he realized how wild he must appear to her. He was shirtless with bare feet and uncombed hair, and his rifle still rested in his hands. Yet she sat prim and proper, appearing not the least intimidated by him. One corner of his mouth rose. The woman had grit.

But now he had to deal with this mixup. This was the second unexpected wrinkle in his plans. The first had been his sharp feeling of regret when he arrived here. To fulfill a promise, after he'd joined the Freedman's Bureau, he'd asked to be assigned to this part of Virginia. He'd expected to feel better coming here—he was, after all, coming home in a way. But upon arrival, he'd felt quite the opposite.

"If the school isn't built yet, what am I to do?" she asked. "I'm supposed to begin lessons for former slaves and their children as soon as feasible. But how can I do that if the school hasn't even been built yet?" A line of worry creased the skin between her ginger eyebrows.

His mouth twisted, a sour taste on his tongue. "It's easy to see what happened. Somebody sent you a letter too early. I'll telegraph the War Department and get this straightened out. You'll just have to go back to where you came from until the school's built."

"We can't go back," she objected. "I have rented out my house for a year."

I work alone, Mrs. Hardy. That's why I took a job where I'd be my own boss. "You can't stay. The school isn't even started—"

She interrupted him again. "We've driven all the way from Pennsylvania."

Joseph cut in, "We're not going to drive all the way back there unless we're going home for good." He'd set his dusty hat on his knee, wiping perspiration from his forehead with a white handkerchief. The little girl stared at Matt like a lost puppy.

Matt frowned at them. They frowned back. He really did not want to deal with this. He rose and walked toward the front window to peer out. Again he detected that subtle shifting in the shadows in front of the house. He stepped near the window and raised his rifle so it would be clearly seen by anyone outside.

Returning here had been a foolish, ill-considered notion. Upon arrival, he'd realized that who he was would just make all the work he had to do here more difficult, more unpleasant, more personal. He muttered too low for anyone else to hear, "I should have gone to Mississippi, where I could have been hated by strangers."

Mrs. Hardy cleared her throat, drawing his attention back to her. She moved to the edge of her seat. "I'm certain that the Freedman's Bureau would not expect an unrelated man and a woman to live under the same roof. Even with my father-in-law living with us…" Her voice drifted into silence.

He couldn't agree more. He heard the nicker of their horses outside again. Did the animals sense something that shouldn't be here? He parted the sheer curtains with his rifle and gazed outside once again.

"I would say that I could find somewhere else in town to stay." He brushed this possibility aside. "But I doubt any of the former Confederate widows would want a Yankee boarding in their homes." *And I wouldn't like it either.* He didn't want to live with others. He hated having to make polite conversation. He hated it now. He continued peering out the window.

"What is distracting thee?" she asked.

He held up one hand and listened, but heard nothing

unusual outside. Still, he asked in a low voice, "You're Quaker, so you didn't come armed, right?"

Joseph spoke up. "Verity's family is Friends. Mind isn't. I brought a gun. Do I need it now?"

Matt watched the shifting of the shadows out in the silver moonlight, concentrating on listening.

"A gun?" she said. "Why would we need—"

Rising, Joseph cut her off. "What's going on here? Haven't the Rebs here heard that Lee's surrendered?"

The woman continued, "Thee didn't tell me thee brought a gun, Joseph."

Matt spoke over her. "Where's the gun?"

The older man came toward him. "It's under the seat on the buckboard, covered with canvas. I wanted it handy if needed."

"Maybe you should go get it now." Matt motioned with his rifle toward the front door. "I'll come out and cover you. And stick to the shadows, but make sure the gun's visible and be sure they hear you checking to see that it's loaded."

Verity stood up quickly. "Wait. Who does thee think is watching us?"

Matt shrugged. "Maybe no one, but I keep seeing shadows shifting outside. And your horses are restless."

"That could be just the wind and the branches," she protested. "I don't want rifles in my house."

"This isn't your house," Matt said, following Joseph to the door. "And some of the Rebs here haven't surrendered. We're from the North and they don't want us here."

She followed them, still balking, "I didn't expect it would be a welcome with open arms—"

He didn't listen to the rest. He shut the front door, closing her inside, and gave cover to Joseph, who collected his gun, making a show of checking to see that it was loaded.

When they reentered the house, the widow stood there with hands on her hips and fire in her eyes. "We don't need guns. We are here to bring healing and hope to this town."

"No, we're not." His patience went up in flames. "We are here to bring change, to stir up trouble. We've come to make people here choke down emancipation and the educating of blacks. The very things they were willing to die to prevent. We've brought a sword, not an olive branch. If you think different, just turn around and leave. No white person is going to want us here. Many will be more than willing to run us out of town. And if they could get away with it, a few would put us under sod in the local churchyard."

His words brought a shocked silence. Then the little girl ran to her mother and buried her face in her mother's skirts. Mrs. Hardy cast him a reproving look and began stroking her daughter's head. Ashamed of upsetting the child, Matt closed and locked the door.

Maybe he had been imagining something or someone lurking outside. But he'd survived the war by learning to distrust everything. "I'm sorry. I didn't mean to… scare her."

"You only spoke the truth," Joseph said. "Christ said He came to bring a sword, not peace. And you knew that, Verity. We discussed it."

"But guns, Joseph," she said in a mournful tone, her voice catching. "The war is over."

Her sad tone stung Matt even more than the little girl's fear. "Why don't we discuss this in the morning?" he said gruffly.

The little girl peered out from her mother's skirts. And then yawned.

Right. Time for bed. A perfect excuse to end the conversation. "It's late," Matt said. "Why don't we just get you settled for the night—"

"But how can we if you're here?" The woman actually blushed.

The solution came to him in a flash. "There is a former slave cabin back by the barn. I'll stay there until this is sorted out. That should fulfill propriety until one of us is moved to another town. We could just take meals together in the house till then. I plan to hire a housekeeper." He felt relief wash over him. He'd keep his privacy and she'd probably get a quick transfer to a more sensible post.

Verity and her father-in-law traded glances. "Are

thee sure thee won't mind?" she asked in a way that told him she wasn't just being polite.

He shrugged. "I lived in tents through the whole war." Images of miserably muddy, bone-chilling nights and cold rain trickling down his neck tried to take him back. He pushed the images and foul sensations aside. "Don't worry about me. The cabin's built solid and has a fireplace. I'll be fine."

"You served in the Union Army, then?" she asked solemnly.

He nodded, giving no expression or comment. *I won't talk about it.*

"My husband served in the Army of the Potomac."

Silence. Matt stared at them, refusing to discuss the war. *It's over. We won. That's all that matters.*

Again, her eyes spoke of her character. Their intensity told him she took very little about this situation lightly. She inhaled deeply, breaking the pregnant moment. "Then we have a workable solution. For now. And tomorrow we'll compose that telegram to the Bureau about this situation. Will thee help us bring in our bedding?"

"Certainly." He moved toward the door, thinking that he didn't like the part about them penning the message together. *I'm quite capable of writing a telegram, ma'am.*

Out in the moonlight, they headed toward the buckboard. Mrs. Hardy walked beside Matt, the top of her head level with his shoulder. She carried herself well. But she kept frowning down at the rifle he carried. And he in turn found his eyes drifting toward hers. "Let's get started carrying your things in, ma'am."

Verity looked up into Matt's eyes. "Thank thee for thy help. I'm sorry we woke thee up and startled thee."

Her direct gaze disrupted his peace. But he found he couldn't look away. There was some quality about her that made him feel... He couldn't come up with the word. He stepped back from her, unhappy with himself. "No apology necessary."

Laying his rifle on the buckboard within easy reach, Matt began helping Joseph untie and roll back the canvas that had protected the boxes and trunks roped securely together on the buckboard.

Maybe this would all be for the best. Maybe he, too, should ask for a transfer in that telegram. It would be wiser. Then he could leave town before Dace and he even came face-to-face. Blood was the tie that had bound them once. But now it was blood spilled in the war that separated them.

His thoughts were interrupted by the gentle sound of Mrs. Hardy sharing a quiet laugh with her daughter. The nearby leaves rustled with the wind and he nearly reached for his rifle. But it was just the wind, wasn't it?

Unsettled. That was the word he'd been looking for. Mrs. Hardy made him feel unsettled. And he didn't like it one bit.

Chapter Two

In the dingy and unfamiliar kitchen, Verity sat at the battered wood table. Her elbows on the bare wood, she gnawed off a chunk of tasteless hardtack. Trying not to gag, she sipped hot black coffee, hoping the liquid would soften the rock in her mouth. Her daughter was too well-behaved to pout about the pitiful breakfast, but her downcast face said it all. Their first breakfast in Fiddlers Grove pretty much expressed their state of affairs—and Verity's feelings about it.

She leaned her forehead against the back of her hand. The house had looked more inviting in moonlight. Gloom crawled up her nape like winding, choking vines. And yet she couldn't keep her disobedient mind from calling up images from the night before—a strong tanned hand gripping a rifle, a broad shoulder sculpted by moonlight.

She gnawed more hardtack. Why had Matthew Ritter behaved as if he'd expected someone to attack them? The war is over. The people here might not like the school, but there is no reason for guns. Her throat rebelled at swallowing more of the gummy slurry. She gagged, trying to hide it from Beth.

Joseph came in the back door. "Ritter isn't in the cabin out back." He sat down and made a face at the hardtack on the plate and the cup of black coffee. Joseph liked bacon, eggs and buttered toast for breakfast, and a lot of cream in his coffee. "Slim pickings, I see."

She sipped more hot coffee and choked down the last of the hardtack. "Yes, I'm going to have to find a farmer and get milk and egg delivery set up. Or perhaps that store in town stocks perishables."

"Do you think we're going to be here long enough to merit that?" Joseph asked. "I'm pretty sure Ritter has gone to the next town to send that telegram."

At the mention of Matthew Ritter, Verity's heart lurched. She looked away, smoothing back the stray hair around her face. Last night when Matthew had opened the door, shirtless and toting a rifle, she hadn't known which shocked her more: his lack of proper dress or the rifle. Of course, they had surprised him after he'd turned in for the night. But he hadn't excused himself and gone to don a shirt or comb his dark hair.

Men often shed their shirts while working in the fields, but he'd sat with them in the parlor shirtless and barefoot. And she couldn't help but notice that Matthew was a fine-looking man. She blocked her mind from bringing up his likeness again. Her deep loneliness, the loneliness she admitted only to the Lord, no doubt prompted this reaction.

As if Joseph had read a bit of her thoughts, he said, "Ritter is probably more comfortable in the company of men. You know, after four long years of army life."

No doubt. She willed away the memory of Matthew Ritter in dishabille. "He might be sending the telegram, but we don't know what the answer will be. Or when it might come." She tried to also dismiss just how completely unwelcoming Matthew Ritter had been. And how blunt. "And we need food because, after all, we're here." *And we can't go back.*

Joseph grunted in agreement. "Well, I'm going to do some work in the barn. This place must have sat empty for quite some time. The paddock fence needs repairs before I dare let the horses out."

Verity rose, forcing herself to face going into a town of strangers. After Matthew's dark forebodings last night, all her own misgivings had flocked to the surface, pecking and squawking like startled chickens. *If we're on the same side, he shouldn't be discouraging me. How will we accomplish anything if we remain at cross-purposes?*

"Joseph, I'm going to walk to the store and see

about buying some food. We'll eat our main meal at midday as usual. I'm sure I'll be able to get what I need to put something simple on the table." *I can do that. This is a state of the Union again. No matter what Matthew said, I will not be afraid of Fiddlers Grove.*

With a nod, Joseph rose. "Little Beth, you going with me or your mom?"

"I want to help in the barn," Beth said, popping up from the table. "May I, Mother?"

"Certainly," Verity said. *Better you should stay here, my sweet girl. I don't want you hurt or frightened. Again.* Last night Matthew's harsh words had caused Beth to run to her. She shivered.

I will not be afraid. Not until I have good reason to be.

With her oak basket over one arm, Verity marched down the dusty road into town. Fiddlers Grove boasted only a group of peeling houses with sagging roofs, two churches and a general store. With the general store looming dead ahead, her feet slowed, growing heavier, clumsier, as if she were treading ankle-deep through thick mud. This town was going to be her home for at least a year. Starting today. *Lord, help me make a good first impression.*

On the bench by the general store's door lounged some older men with unshaven, dried-apple faces. Matthew's warning that some here would welcome her death made her quiver, but she inhaled and then smiled at them.

Grime coated the storefront windows with a fine film and the door stood propped open. Flies buzzed in and out. Her pulse hopping and skipping, Verity nodded at the older men who'd risen respectfully as she passed them. She crossed the threshold.

A marked hush fell over the store. Every eye turned to her. Drawing in as much air as she could, Verity walked like a stick figure toward the counter. The townspeople fell back, leaving her alone in the center of the sad and bare-looking store. She halted, unable to go forward.

She began silently reciting the twenty-third psalm, an old habit in the midst of stress. *The Lord is my shepherd; I shall not want. He maketh me to lie down in green pastures: He leadeth me beside the still waters.*

Near the counter, a slight woman in a frayed bonnet and patched dress edged away from Verity, joining the surrounding gawkers. Verity tried to act naturally, letting everyone stare at her as if she hadn't fastened her buttons correctly.

She forced her legs to carry her forward. "Good morning," she greeted the proprietor. Her voice trembled, giving her away.

The thin, graying man behind the counter straightened. "Good day, ma'am. I'm Phil Hanley, the storekeeper. What may I do for you?"

She acknowledged his introduction with a wobbly nod, intense gazes still pressing in on her from all sides. Her smile felt tight and false, like the grin stitched on a rag doll's face.

"Phil Hanley, I'm Verity Hardy and I need some of those eggs." She indicated a box of brown eggs on the counter. "And, if thee have any, some bacon. And I need to ask thee who sells milk in town. I require at least two quarts a day. And I'm out of bread. I'll need to set up my kitchen before I begin baking bread again." Her words had spilled out in a rapid stream, faster than usual.

In the total silence that followed, the man stared at her as if she'd been speaking a foreign language. People who weren't used to Plain Speech often did this, she told herself. They would soon grow accustomed—if she and her family stayed here longer than Matthew hoped.

She waited, perspiring. As the silence continued, Verity blotted her upper lip with a handkerchief from her apron pocket. More of the twenty-third psalm played in her mind. *For Thou art with me; Thy rod and Thy staff they comfort me.*

"Ma'am." A slight, pinched-looking woman edged nearer and offered in a hesitant voice, "I just baked this mornin'. I have a spare pan of cornbread."

With a giddy rush of gratitude, Verity turned toward the woman. "Thank thee. I'm Verity Hardy. And thee is?"

"Mary. I mean, Mrs. Orrin Dyke, ma'am." Mary curtsied.

"I'm pleased to meet thee." Verity offered her hand like a man instead of curtsying like a woman, knowing this would also brand her as an oddity. *Well, in for a penny, in for a pound.*

Mary Dyke shook her hand tentatively.

"Mary Dyke, I'm living at the Barnesworth house. Could thee drop by with that cornbread later this morning?"

"Yes, ma'am. I can do that," Mary said with a shy blush, curtsying again.

Verity reached into her pocket and then held out a coin. "Here. I'll pay thee in advance."

"No." Mary backed away, one ungloved hand up. "You just give the money to Mr. Hanley to put on my account. I'll bring the bread over right away. 'Sides, that's way too much for a pan of bread. I couldn't take more than a nickel."

Sensing a stiffening in the people surrounding her, Verity wondered how she'd given offense. Still, she held out the dime, her mind racing as she tried to come up with a way to make her offer acceptable. "But I'll owe thee for delivery, too."

"No, no, ma'am, I can't take anything for bringing it. Or in advance." Mary scurried from the store.

Verity appeared to have offended the woman by offering to pay too much and in advance. But what could she do to amend that here and now? Nothing. Her mind went back to the psalm. *He restoreth my soul.* Yes, please, Lord, she thought. She took a deep breath and said through dry lips that were trying to stick together, "Two dozen of those fine brown eggs, please, Phil Hanley?"

"Of course." He set the offered oak basket on the counter and carefully wrapped the eggs in newspaper, nestling them into it. His movements provided the only sound in the store other than Verity's audible rapid breathing. She fought the urge to fidget.

"Anything else, ma'am?"

"Well, now that I'm going to have cornbread—" she smiled "—I'll need butter. And the bacon, if thee has some. Two pounds, please?"

"Just a moment." He stepped out the back door, leaving Verity on display. While she gazed at the nearly empty shelves, the crowd surrounding her gawked in stolid suspicion. The feeling that she was on a stage and had just forgotten her lines washed through her, cold then hot. *Thou preparest a table before me in the presence of mine enemies.*

In the persistent silence, the storeowner reentered and wrapped the butter and slab of bacon with the rustling of more newspaper. He tucked them into her basket. "Anything else, ma'am?"

"Not right now. How much do I owe thee?" The thought that her ordeal was almost over made her fingers fumble. But finally, out of her dangling reticule, she pulled a leather purse. She struggled with the catch, and then opened it. The taut silence flared and she sensed their disapproval distinctly. She glanced around and saw that everyone was staring at the U.S. greenbacks folded neatly in her purse.

She pressed her dry lips together. A show of wealth was always distasteful, especially in the presence of such lean, ragged people. She tasted bitter regret. At every turn, she appeared unable to stop offending these people. *Lord, help me. I'm doing everything wrong.*

The proprietor spoke up, breaking the uncomfortable silence. "After Mary's nickel for the bread, that's just two bits then, ma'am."

She gave him the coins. "I'll bid thee good day then, Phil Hanley." She offered him her gloved hand.

He shook it and nodded farewell. Still smiling her rag-doll smile, she walked out into the bright sunlight.

Cool relief began to trickle through her. She'd gotten food for the midday meal and let Fiddlers Grove know she'd arrived. It said much about the suffering of Virginia that she, who'd always lived a simple life, should suddenly have to be concerned about flaunting wealth. Wounding Southern pride wouldn't help her in her work here. She'd have to be more careful. *I'd never had been this jumpy if Matthew Ritter hadn't tried to scare me off. It won't happen again, Lord, with Thy help.*

* * *

Later that warm, bright morning, Verity stood at the door of her new home, her pulse suddenly galloping. "Won't thee come in, Mary Dyke?" *Lord, help me say the right things.*

"No, ma'am. Here's your pan of bread, as promised." The small woman's eyes flitted around as if she were afraid. She handed Verity the circle of cornbread, wrapped within a ragged but spotless kitchen cloth. A sandy-haired boy who looked to be about eleven had accompanied Mary Dyke.

Verity needed information about the sad-looking town and its people to get a sense of how the community would really react to the new school. In spite of Matthew's warning, Verity refused to assume the possibility of community cooperation was impossible.

Verity smiled. "Mary, I've never moved before— at least, not since I married and left home to move into my husband's house. I was wondering if thee…and is this thy son?"

"Yes, ma'am." A momentary smile lit the woman's drawn face. Mrs. Dyke patted her son's shoulder. He was taller than his mother already and very thin, with a sensitive-looking face. "This is my son, Alec. Son, make your bow."

The boy obeyed his mother and then Verity felt a tug at her own skirt and looked down. Evidently Beth had been drawn by the lure of another child. "This is my daughter. Beth, this is Mary Dyke and her son, Alec." Her seven-year-old daughter with long dark braids and a serious face made a curtsy, and stole a quick glance at the boy.

"What is it you are wondering about, ma'am?" Mary Dyke asked, sounding wary.

"I could use some help opening boxes and putting away my kitchen things." Verity gestured toward the chaotic room behind her. "Would thee have time to help me unpack boxes? I'm sure company would make the work go faster." *Please, Lord, help me make a friend here.*

The woman appeared uneasy, but then bit her lip and said, "I can stay a mite longer."

"Excellent. And perhaps thy son would like to help my father-in-law with the horses in the barn?" All children loved horses—and Joseph.

"Yes, ma'am." Alec bowed again and started toward the barn at the back of the property. Beth slipped from her mother's side and followed the boy, keeping a safe distance from him.

Verity smiled and ushered Mary into her disordered kitchen. Wooden boxes with straw and crumpled newspaper packing covered the floor. "Thee sees what I mean?"

"Yes, ma'am."

Soon Verity and Mary were working side by side. Unwrapping jars of preserves swathed in newsprint,

Verity was cheered by Mary Dyke's companionship. She already missed her six sisters back in Pennsylvania and her kind neighbors. If she were to be able to accomplish both her public and private reasons for coming here, she needed to begin to learn about the people here. And she couldn't forget that she'd come with a personal mission, too.

Then Verity asked a question that had occurred to her on the way home. "Where is the school? I didn't see it in town. I want to get Beth enrolled." Verity paused to blot the perspiration on her forehead with a white handkerchief from her apron pocket.

Mary didn't glance up. "Ma'am, we don't have a school in town."

"No school?" Verity couldn't keep the dismayed surprise out of her tone.

"I've heard that there are free schools in the North," Mary commented in a flat tone, not meeting Verity's eyes.

Verity realized she'd just insulted the town again. She racked her brain, trying to think of some way to open up this timid woman—not to gossip but merely to provide Verity with helpful information.

Perhaps honesty would suffice. "I'm afraid that I offended many at the store this morning. I didn't mean to, but perhaps I should have been less forward with my offer of payment. I hope I didn't offend thee by offering to pay thee to deliver the bread."

When no reply came, Verity's face warmed with embarrassment. "It's just that I don't know anyone here yet and I didn't want to… I don't know exactly how to say what I mean. I just didn't want thee to think thee owed me anything. If we were back in Pennsylvania, I would probably have known thee all my life…" *Why can't I stop babbling?* "Oh, I'm doing a terrible job of explaining."

Mary finally glanced her way. "No, ma'am, I think I understand and I wasn't offended—or maybe I should say not much. You're a Yankee, and I know Yankees don't have Southern manners." Then the woman colored red. "I mean—"

Verity chuckled. "Now thee knows how I feel. And thee hasn't offended me."

The back door swung open and Matthew Ritter stepped inside. "Mary!" he exclaimed.

In the midst of lifting a jar of peaches to the shelf, Mary dropped it. The glass shattered, the yellow fruit and syrups splattering the floor, wall and Mary's skirts. "Oh, ma'am, I'm so sorry!"

Matthew stood apart, saying nothing. Seeing Mary prompted scenes from childhood to flood his mind—playing hide and seek among the ancient oaks around Mary's house, fishing at the creek, running in the fields with Dace and Samuel. Why did the widow have to be here as witness to the first time he encountered an old friend who was now probably an enemy?

When the mess had been cleaned up, he took a deep breath and said, "I'm sorry I startled you, Mary." He wondered for a moment if she would try to act as if she didn't know him.

Mary turned toward him, but looked at the floor. "That's all right, Matt. I just didn't expect to see you here. Someone said they thought they'd seen you, but…"

A strained silence stretched between them. A string of odd reactions hit him—his throat was thick, his eyes smarted, he felt hot and then cold. To break the unbearable silence, he nodded toward her simple gold wedding band. "You're married, I see."

She still wouldn't meet his gaze. "Yes, I married Orrin Dyke. We have one son, Alec."

Orrin Dyke? Sweet Mary McKay had married that shiftless oaf, Matt hoped his low opinion of her husband didn't show on his face. He forced words through his dry throat, "I'm happy to hear that."

Mary looked up then. "Are you… Have you come home for good?"

Home for good? The thought sliced like a bayonet. He grimaced. "Probably not. I doubt I'll be welcome here." He made himself go on and tell the truth, the whole truth. "I'm working for the Freedman's Bureau. I'm here to help former slaves adjust to freedom and prepare them to vote."

Mary simply stared at him.

He'd expected his job to be offensive to his old friends, but he was who he was.

The Quaker widow watched them in silence. Her copper hair and air of confidence contrasted sharply with Mary's meek and shabby appearance. Meeting Mary after all these years was hard enough without the widow taking in every word, every expression. His face and neck warmed—he hated betraying his strong reaction to the situation.

"Your parents?" Mary asked.

He swallowed down the gorge that had risen in his throat. "My parents died during the war."

"I'm sorry." And Mary did sound sorry.

"Your parents?" he asked, wishing the widow would excuse herself and leave them. But of course, it would be almost improper for her to do so.

"My mother died, but Pa's still alive. It's good to see you again, Matt, safe and sound after the war."

He imagined all the prickly thoughts that might be coursing through Mary's mind about his fighting on the Union side and the reason his family had left town in 1852. Just thinking of leaving Fiddlers Grove brought back the same sinking feeling it had that day in 1852—as if the floor had opened and was swallowing him inch by inch.

Mary turned to the widow. "Ma'am, I must be leaving."

"Of course, Mary Dyke, I thank thee for thy help." The widow shook Mary's hand as if she were a man.

Matt held on to his composure as he bowed, wishing Mary goodbye.

Mary curtsied and then she was out the back door, calling, "Alec!" Her son, Orrin's son.

That left him alone with the widow as they faced each other in the kitchen. Again, he was struck by her unruly copper curls, which didn't fit her serene yet concerned expression. He wanted to turn and leave. But of course, he had to deal with her. He took himself in hand. *I faced cannon so I can face this inquisitive woman and my hometown where I won't be welcome.*

She went to the stove and lifted the coffeepot there. "Would thee like a cup?"

He wanted to refuse and leave, but he was thirsty and they needed to talk. He hoped she didn't make good coffee. He didn't want to like anything about this woman. He forced out a gruff "Please."

She motioned him to sit at the table and served him the coffee. Then she sat down facing him. "I take it that thee went to send the telegram about our situation?"

He'd braced himself for her expected interrogation. "Yes, I did, and I bought some chickens for the yard and a cow for milk."

She raised her eyebrows at him. "I'm surprised that thee made these purchases. Thee sounded last night as if thee didn't think my family and I would be here long enough to merit the purchase of any stock."

He sipped the hot coffee. It was irritatingly good. "I'll be here long enough to do what I signed on to do." That much he'd decided on his ride to send the telegram. "And whether you're here or not, I'll need eggs and milk. We need to hire a housekeeper. Would you do that? Hire her?"

The woman considered him for a few moments. "I could do that. But perhaps I should just do the house-keeping until I start teaching."

He shook his head. He didn't want this woman to become someone he'd come to depend on. With any luck, she'd be gone soon. "When you're busy teach-ing, it would be better to have household help." It wasn't shading the truth, since the decision as to whether she would stay or go was not up to him. After all, he might end up stuck with this woman indefi-nitely. With her early arrival the Freedman's Bureau had demonstrated that it could make mistakes.

"Very well. I'll see about hiring a housekeeper."

He sipped more of her good coffee, brooding over all he couldn't change in the situation. After four years of following orders, he'd wanted to be free, on his own. And then here she was. And then the question he dreaded came.

"Thee didn't tell me that thee had ever lived here before."

Yes, I didn't, and I don't want to tell you now. "I lived here with my parents until I was around twelve. Then we moved to New York State." *And that's all you need to know.*

"I see."

Was she too polite to ask why? He waited. Evidently she was. *Good.* Feeling suddenly freer, he rose. "I'm going out to settle the stock. I see your father-in-law is already working on that fence that needed fixing."

"Yes, Joseph is very handy to have around. When it's time for dinner, I'll ring the bell. I bought only bacon, eggs and cornbread, so the menu will be somewhat limited. But soon I'll have the kitchen completely stocked, and with a cow and some chickens, we'll only need to buy meat and greens from a local farmer."

Matt nodded and walked outside into the hot sunshine. As he stood there, the muscles in his neck tightened. He remembered the look on Mary's face when she'd recognized him. Well, the fat would sizzle soon. Word that he was indeed back in town would whip through Fiddlers Grove like a tornado. It couldn't be avoided. But he'd given his word and he'd stand by it.

The concerned look the widow had given him poured acid on his already lacerated nerves. He wanted no sympathy—just to do his work and move on. Oh, he hoped that telegram would come soon. He wanted this disturbing Quaker widow anywhere but here.

* * *

Later that afternoon, Verity was putting the final touches on the freshly hemmed and pressed white kitchen curtains she'd had sense enough to bring. When someone knocked on her back door, she started. Scolding herself for lingering jitters, she went to open the door and found a tall, sturdily built black woman looking back at her.

Her visitor appeared to be in her middle years with the beginning of silver hair around the edges of a red kerchief tied at the front of her head.

"May I help thee?"

"I'm Hannah. I've come to meet y'all Yankees."

The woman's directness made Verity smile, and some of the tightness inside her eased. "Please come in, Hannah. I'm Verity Hardy."

"Are you a Miss or Mrs.?" The woman looked at her pointedly.

"I'm a widow, but I'm a Quaker and prefer to be called by name." Verity opened the door and gestured the woman in. *Please, Lord, help me do better with this new neighbor.*

"Yes, ma'am." The woman entered the kitchen.

Footsteps sounded in the hall and Beth ran into the kitchen. She halted at the sight of Hannah.

"Hello." Beth curtsied. "I'm Beth."

"You can call me Aunt Hannah, you sweet child." The woman's face and voice softened.

Beth looked to her mother for direction. Verity nodded. "If the woman wishes to be called Aunt Hannah, Beth, thee may address her in that way." Then she turned Hannah. "Won't thee sit down? I have coffee on the stove."

Hannah stared at her and then at the table. "This Virginia. Whites and blacks don't never sit down together."

Verity did not know what to say to this. It made her stomach flutter.

"But we're not from Virginia," Beth explained earnestly.

Hannah laughed. "You sure ain't, honey. I know that. Tell you what, I go back outside and set on the top step and you can bring me that cup of coffee. And y'all can sit on chairs on the back porch. And that would look all right. How's that?"

Verity nodded in agreement. Why had Hannah come? Was she bringing more bad news? Very soon, the three of them were seated in Hannah's suggested manner on the small back porch. Verity waited for Hannah to speak. She hated this awkwardness, this unfamiliarity—hated being the stranger. Odd tremors had coursed through her on and off ever since her trip to town. Now they started up again, making her feel off balance.

After several sips of coffee, Hannah began, "I hear you folks come from the North and you talk like

Quakers. And I figure if you be a Quaker, then I think afore the war you was abolitionist, too."

"Yes, my whole family was very active in the abolitionist movement," Verity replied. *Where was this leading?*

Hannah nodded. "I figured so. What're y'all doing here in Fiddlers Grove, then?"

Only God knows the full answer to that. "I came to teach school."

"What school?"

"The school Matthew Ritter is here to build."

Hannah stared at her. "I heard the Ritter boy come back."

"Yes, he has." So Matthew was generally known here. Verity tried to discern what Hannah's attitude was toward the man's return, but Hannah's reaction was not apparent.

"What you two living here together for? Are you married?"

Verity sighed silently and tried to quell the trembling that wouldn't leave her. The close living arrangement with Matthew would be a topic of gossip and speculation, so she might as well tell this woman. She explained the mistake about her coming too soon and Matthew moving to the cabin. Hoping to sidestep the queries and pick up some information, Verity continued, "May I ask thee a question?"

Hannah nodded.

"Soon it will be First Day. And I see that thee has but two churches in town—"

"First day, what that?" Hannah looked puzzled.

"Quakers use Plain Speech, meaning we try to speak simply and truthfully. We do not use the same names for the days of the week as other Christians do because each one of them is named after a pagan god."

"I never knew that."

Beth piped up, "Wednesday is from Woden. He was a Nordic god."

"Do tell," Hannah replied with a grin.

Verity chuckled, but pressed on, "I was inquiring about the churches—"

"We got St. John's and Fiddlers Grove Community," Hannah said.

"Which church does thee worship at?" Verity asked, setting down her cup carefully so as not to let it rattle on the saucer.

"Neither. I attend Brother Elijah's preaching on the Ransford place on Sunday afternoons. Elijah is the Ransford butler and my husband."

Verity nodded. "I see. Does either town church have an evening service?"

"Fiddlers Grove Community has 6:30 p.m. service. But St. John's only meet at 9:00 a.m. sharp. They got a bell. Y'all hear it, all right."

"Thank you, Hannah." Verity waited, sensing the

woman was finally about to reveal her reason for coming.

Hannah put her empty cup down on the step. She bowed her head for a moment and then looked up at Verity. "I can't read or write. Can you write me a letter? I know the name and a place to send it. I can pay."

The request pricked Verity's heart. *How awful not to be able to read and write. Lord, help me get this school started here or wherever Thee wishes.* "I have time to write a letter. And I would take it as a kindness if thee would let me do it for thee without pay. I don't think it's right to charge a neighbor."

Hannah grinned. "I thank you. Will you write that letter for me now?"

"Certainly." Verity rose and dragged her chair back inside, leading the way for her daughter and Hannah to follow. "Who am I writing to?"

"The name's Isaiah Watson and he live in Buffalo, New York."

"Is this a matter of business?" Verity asked.

"Don't know if you'd call this business or not. There be someone I want to find. And I think Mr. Isaiah Watson might know where that person be."

"Aunt Hannah," Beth asked, "who is the person that you want to find?"

"Miss Beth, I want to find my boy."

Chapter Three

In the dazzling light of First Day, Verity gazed at St. John's Church, which sat on a gentle rise in the midst of an oak grove at the edge of town. It was small but impressive with its tall steeple and golden marigolds along its cobblestone path. Her father-in-law and Beth walked beside her, through the red door and into the sudden dimness of the church foyer. Matthew brought up the rear. A very grim and reluctant Matthew.

She hoped that three visits to three churches would remind the people of Fiddlers Grove that they shared a common faith in Christ. Still, her spine had become a tightly wound spring she couldn't relax. She feared that this would be worse than visiting the store. Quakers never called attention to themselves—never. And worst of all, the fear Matthew had sparked within her lingered.

Inside St. John's, a pipe organ began playing. Beth did a little jump. "Music."

Verity smiled, though her lips felt stiff. Beth shared her late father's love of music. Verity waited until the congregation had finished the first verse, then she nodded at Joseph and Matthew. Joseph led them down the center aisle to seats in an empty pew near the back of the church. Matthew removed his hat and stood beside Verity, taking the aisle space. He hadn't brought his rifle, of course, but he looked as forbidding as if he had. It was almost as if he expected someone to attack them.

As expected, many heads swiveled to watch them enter. Verity smiled, her lips wooden. Then Beth began to sing along, as did Joseph. Their voices—the high wispy soprano and the low bass—blended in with the singing. "'Lord, as to Thy dear cross we flee, and plead to be forgiven.'" She hoped the people singing were listening to the words coming from their mouths. "'Kept peaceful in the midst of strife, forgiving and forgiven, O may we lead the pilgrim's life, and follow Thee to heaven.'"

Quaker meetings were composed of silence, praying and speaking, not singing. Though Verity didn't feel comfortable singing, she enjoyed the music, which calmed her wary heart and lifted her spirit. Still, Matthew stood beside her as stiff and silent as a sentinel. Waves of infectious tension wafted from him.

But his formidable presence also managed to reassure her. No one would antagonize Matthew Ritter without good reason.

Verity looked up over her shoulder and saw what must have been a slaves' balcony. It was empty now, showing that—after emancipation—the black population must not want to come to the white man's church.

The hymn ended. There was a general rustling around the church as books were put back into their holders and ladies gathered their skirts to sit down. Verity concentrated on the vicar, who in his clerical collar and vestments looked about the same age as her father-in-law. Then she noted that one man, who looked to be about Matthew's age, kept glancing back at her and Matthew.

Throughout the rest of the service, Verity tried to ignore the surreptitious glances from the people of Fiddlers Grove. It was no surprise that people would be curious about them; still, it made her uneasy. Who was the one man who looked at Matthew over and over?

After the final hymn was sung, the congregation rose and made its way into the aisle. Verity, Joseph, Beth and Matthew made their way toward the clergyman, standing at the doorway and shaking hands with everyone as they left.

She was very aware of the same man who'd kept glancing at Matthew. Was he planning on making trouble? Matthew, on the other hand, pointedly ignored the man.

When it was finally her turn to offer her hand to the vicar, it felt as if the whole congregation on the steps and in the foyer paused and fell silent, listening. Verity swallowed and tried to smile.

"Good morning," the vicar said. "I am Pastor Savage."

"That's a scary name," Beth said.

Verity touched her daughter's shoulder. Beth hung her head and then curtsied. "I beg your pardon."

"Mine is an unusual name, especially for a clergyman." Pastor Savage smiled. "You are new to Fiddlers Grove."

"Yes," Joseph responded, and shook the pastor's hand.

"Everyone has been wondering why you have come to our little town. Many believe you are one of those meddling Yankee schoolmarms we've heard of." His tone was friendly but uncertain.

"It is hard to be a stranger in a small town," Verity said without giving him an answer. She liked the pastor's eyes. They were good eyes. But very sad ones, too.

"Maybe our new family moved to Fiddlers Grove for their health," a pretty woman in a once stylish but now faded dress suggested in a sly tone. She stood beside the man who'd been watching Matthew.

Verity smiled, though a frisson of fear went through her. Had there been a veiled threat in that statement?

Would it be "unhealthy" here for them? There was a pregnant pause while everyone waited for Verity to reply.

When she did not, the man beside the woman said, "May I make myself known to you? This is my wife, Lirit, and I'm Dacian Ransford. I wish to welcome you to our town."

Mr. Ransford must have served in the Confederate Army. He had that "starved and marched too long" look she'd seen so often in '63. "I am pleased to meet thee," she murmured, for once not really sure she meant her proper words. It was obvious in the way Dacian dressed that he was a prominent member of society here. Hadn't Hannah said that her husband was the Ransford butler?

Joseph accepted Dacian Ransford's hand and Beth curtsied. Then before Joseph could introduce the fourth member of their party, the man faced Matthew. "Hello, Matt."

"Dace." Matthew nodded, no emotion visible on his face.

"I didn't expect to see you in Fiddlers Grove again." Neither Dacian Ransford's tone nor his expression gave any clue as to whether he thought it good or bad to see Matthew here now. Yet neither offered a hand to the other.

Verity tried to behave as if she were unaware of the heightened tension that ran through the milling con-gregation. Matthew's expression became stony.

"Oh?" Matt replied. No emotion. No inflection.

Perhaps war did this to men; perhaps it "closed" them. Suddenly she wondered why Matthew's family had left Fiddlers Grove.

As Verity studied the two men, a forceful wind moved her skirts. Overhead, large white clouds glided across the blue sky.

"How is my aunt Samantha?" Dacian asked Matthew.

"My mother died of cholera in '62. She had been widowed for a year then. And my aunt Sarah Rose?" Matthew asked.

"My mother passed just after Lincoln was elected. A fever. My father survived her by two years."

"I'm sorry to hear that," Matthew said, sounding sincere.

"And I'm sorry also about your parents passing." The two men were silent for a moment, and then Dacian nodded and took his wife's elbow, steering her down the church steps.

Verity tried to make sense of this exchange between first cousins, as well as the shocking news she'd gathered—the fact that Matthew hadn't mentioned Dacian. Why hadn't Matthew just told them he had relatives in town?

Later that day, Matthew trailed after Verity and her family, heading toward the singing coming from a maple-and-oak grove on the Ransford plantation. Why had the Quaker insisted they attend three church services today? She'd only smiled when he'd asked her. He was tempted to stay behind, but he hadn't wanted her going without him. And of course, he'd come face-to-face with Dace this morning. His emotions from that meeting continued to bubble up inside him. He crammed them down. *Forget it. Forget all of it.*

The singing drew them closer and he began to recognize many of the black faces as people from his childhood. He tightened his defenses against all this remembering. Yet he still searched for Samuel's face. From him, he might get a genuine welcome.

Before emancipation, slaves had been required to attend church with their masters. Now they were holding their own service and singing a popular freedom song he'd heard in the streets of Richmond and Washington D.C.

Mammy, don't yo' cook and sew no mo'.
Yo' are free, yo' are free.
Rooster, don't you crow no mo'.
Yo' are free, yo' are free.
Old hen, don't yo' lay no mo' eggs.
Yo' are free, yo' are free.

At sight of them, the whole congregation broke off in the middle of a note and fell silent. Abashed, the widow's little girl hung back, hiding within the folds of her mother's skirt. The boisterous wind that had come up this morning was now picking up more speed. The black ribbons of the Quaker's bonnet flared in the wind. Verity smiled, looking untroubled and genuine. But was anyone that cool? What would stir this woman enough to pierce her outward calm? Or did it go straight through to her very core?

Matt had eaten the cold midday meal with them, but hadn't offered any explanation about his past in Fiddlers Grove. Why couldn't he just tell her why his family had left and why he'd come back? Somehow, explanations remained impossible.

He recognized Hannah in the shade of a twisted old oak and felt a pang. Samuel's mother had survived. She hurried to him and hugged him. "Mr. Matt, welcome home."

"Mr. Matt!" Hannah's husband, Elijah, grasped both Matt's hands. "I heard that you had come back to town. As I live and breathe, sir. As I live and breathe."

"It's good to see you, too, Elijah." Matt swallowed down all the memories that were forcing their way up from deep inside him. He wanted so much to ask about Samuel, but he found he couldn't say the name.

Elijah visibly pulled himself together. "Yes, welcome home, Mr. Matt." The man's genuine warmth had been so unexpected that Matt glanced skyward, hiding his reaction.

It struck him that Elijah wasn't quite as tall as Matt

remembered him. Perhaps because Matt had been a child the last time he'd seen Elijah. Elijah looked gaunt, and his closely cropped hair and bushy eyebrows were threaded with silver. He was dressed in a good-quality but worn suit and spoke with a cultured cadence. After all, he was the Ransfords' butler.

Again Matt felt the urge to ask where Samuel was. But what if Samuel had died? He couldn't bring himself to stir those waters.

"Y'all come just like you said you would." Hannah approached Verity and offered her a work-worn hand. "I told everybody about how you wrote that letter for me."

What letter? To whom? Matt's heart started throbbing in his chest. *What was the woman up to now?*

Verity shook Hannah's hand. "It was a pleasure to help thee. Hannah, thee remembers my daughter, Beth. And this is my father-in-law, Joseph Hardy."

Hannah introduced Verity and her family to Elijah. "Sister Verity, we're glad to have you and your family. Welcome," he said.

"I ain't glad," declared a large woman wearing a patterned indigo kerchief over her hair. "Do the Ransfords know this Ritter boy back in town? And what a white woman and her folks doin' comin' here? I want to know if she with the Freedman's Bureau. And when we going to get our land? That's the only reason I stayed in this place—to get what's due me."

"I told you they was Quakers and abolitionists afore

the war." Hannah propped her hands on her ample hips. "And why shouldn't the Ritter boy come home?"

Come home. Matt was undone. Blinking away tears, he stared up into the gray clouds flying in from the northeast.

The woman with the indigo kerchief demanded, "Are they are our side or master side?"

"We are on God's side, I hope," Verity said. "I wish thee will all go on with thy singing, Elijah."

Matt glanced at her out of the corner of his eye. *Thank you.* Hannah urged the widow and her family to take seats on the large downed log in the shade. Matt hung back, leaning against an elm. The brim of the widow's bonnet flapped in the wind, giving him glimpses of her long, golden-brown lashes against her fair cheek.

Soon, the congregation was singing and clapping to "O Mary."

"O Mary, don't you weep, don't you mourn
O Mary, don't you weep, don't you mourn,
Pharaoh's army got drowned."

Matt wondered if, in their minds, Pharaoh's army was the Army of the Confederacy. It had gone down in defeat like Pharaoh's army. But it hadn't been an easy defeat. Why was it that he could stand here in the sun listening to beautiful singing and yet still be on the battlefield, with cannons blasting him to deafness? Why wouldn't his mind just let go of the war?

"O Mary, don't you weep
Some of these mornings bright and fair
Take my wings and cleave the air
Pharaoh's army got drowned.
O Mary, don't you weep.
When I get to heaven goin' to sing and shout
Nobody there for to turn me out."

The little girl was singing and clapping with the gathering. Her mother sat quiet and ladylike, her gloved hands folded in her lap. Her serenity soothed something in Matt. He tried not to stare, but drew his gaze away with difficulty.

He repeated the words of the song in his mind. *Some of these mornings bright and fair, Take my wings and cleave the air.*

Though his heavy burden of memories tried to drag him down, he fought to focus on the present. The work his parents had begun must be completed. The laws of the land must be the same for white and black. He must not lose sight of that.

The widow glanced over her shoulder at him. How long could he hold back from telling her the story of his family and Fiddlers Grove? The simple answer was that he could not ignore Dace—not just because

Dace was his only cousin, but also because Dace had the power to sway others. The Ransfords had run this town for over a hundred years. Matt came to a decision. He'd have to talk to Dace. There was always an outside chance that Dace wouldn't be hostile to the school, wasn't there?

After the evening meal, Matt trudged through the wild wind into the white frame church with Verity and her family. The church sat at the end of the town's main street. It was surrounded by oaks, elms and maples and was much larger than St. John's. The wind tugged at Matt's hat. A storm was certain. Matt looked forward to it, hoping for relief from the stifling, unseasonal heat of the past few days.

On the other hand, Matt dreaded walking into this church. Most of its members had been vocal enemies of his parents. And Matt wondered which of them had been responsible for that final night that had sent his family north. His gut clenched. He reminded himself that that was all past and his side had won the war. Not theirs.

Again they entered during the opening hymn. They elicited glances, some surreptitious and some blatant. Toward the front, Mary and her son, Alec, sat with her father, Jed McKay, who looked like an Old Testament prophet. Orrin was nowhere in sight—an unexpected blessing.

When the hymn ended, the preacher looked

straight at them and demanded, "What are you people here for?"

For once, the widow looked startled. "I beg thy pardon?"

"We don't want Yankees coming down here and telling us what to do with our people. If you're here to do that, you might as well leave in the morning. We won't tolerate any Yankee meddling."

Matt waited to see what the Quaker would say before he entered the fray.

"Friend, I am not a meddler. But anyone who thinks nothing here is going to change after secession, four years of bloodshed, Lee's surrender and emancipation is deluding themselves."

Matt's eyes widened. The widow's tone was civil but her words broadsided the congregation. He felt the angry response slap back at them. *Whoa.* The woman had nerve, that was for certain.

Jed McKay leaped to his feet and pointed a finger at her. "We're not going to let a bunch of Yankees tell us how to run things in Fiddlers Grove."

"What things are thee talking about, Friend?" the widow asked, as if only politely interested.

Matt's respect for her was rising. A grin tugged at a corner of his mouth.

Jed swallowed a couple of times and then came back with, "We won't have our darkies learning how to read and such. And they'll never vote in Virginia.

Never. Blacks voting is just as far-fetched and outlandish as letting women vote. Won't happen. No, sir."

"Does thee not read the papers?" the widow countered in a courteous voice. "The Congress is waiting for the amendment for Negro suffrage to be passed by the states, and when it is, Negroes will vote in Virginia."

"Over my dead body!" Jed roared.

"I believe, Friend," the widow replied in a tranquil tone, "that there has been enough bloodshed. And I hope many will agree with me."

Matt drew in a deep breath at her audacity. *Whoa.*

Her words left Jed with nothing coherent to say. He grumbled mutinously and then looked at Matt. "Ritter, you should never have come back here. That's all I got to say to you." With this, Jed sat down.

"I think it would be best if you all leave our service," the preacher said. "Now."

"Mother, can he make us leave church? I thought anybody could go to church," Beth said in a stage whisper, tugging at her mother's sleeve.

Matt looked to Verity, leaving it to her whether they stayed or left. After all, this had been her idea. But he'd take on the whole congregation if she wanted him to. In fact, his hands were already balled into fists.

"I bid thee good evening, then," Verity said, taking Beth's hand and walking into the aisle like the lady she was. Matt followed her to the door of the church. Then he turned back and gave the congregation a look that declared, Everything the lady said is true. We'll leave now. I don't listen to a preacher who speaks hate. This isn't over.

The wind hurried them all home, billowing the widow's skirt and making Joseph and Matt hold on to their hats. At their back door he paused for a moment, thinking yet again that he should say something about Fiddlers Grove and his family, but he could come up with nothing he wished to say. So he bid them good-night and headed for the cabin. Behind him, he heard Verity and her father-in-law closing and latching the windows against the coming storm.

Just before Matt closed the cabin door, he gazed up at the storm-darkened sky. Jed McKay's words came back: "Ritter, you should never have come back here." Opposition was a funny thing. Initially, he'd felt the same way as McKay—that he shouldn't have come back. But now that he'd been run out of one church, rebellion tightened in his gut. *No one's running me out of town. Not again.*

The thunder awakened Verity. And Beth's scream. Verity leaped out of bed. Lightning flashed, flickering like noonday sunshine, illuminating the room. Beth ran into the room and threw her arms around her mother. "Make it stop! Make it stop!"

Verity recognized the hysteria in her daughter's

voice. Thunder always brought back their shared fear of loud noises that had begun with the cannon at Gettysburg and the terror of war. Verity knew from experience that words would not help Beth. She wrapped her arms around her daughter, hugging her fiercely. That was the only thing that ever helped. Verity's own heart pounded in tune with the relentless thunder.

Then the house shook. And exploded.

Or that was what it sounded like. Felt like.

Joseph charged into her room, trousers over his nightshirt. "I think we've been hit by lightning," he shouted over the continuing din. "I'm going outside to see if anything caught fire."

Verity glanced out the window and shrieked, "The barn! The barn's on fire!"

Joseph ran from the room. Verity settled Beth in her bed and pulled the blankets up over the child. "Stay here, Beth. I must help thy grandfather!"

Verity snatched up her robe, trying not to hear her daughter's frightened cries as she ran. Outside, the storm shook the night. Lightning blazed. Thunder pounded. Barefoot on the coarse wet grass, Verity ran with her hands over her ears. It seemed impossible that anything could burn in the downpour, yet flames flashed inside the open barn loft.

Ahead, Joseph and Matthew were opening the stalls to get the horses out of the burning barn. Between thunderclaps, the shrieking of horses slashed the night.

Verity raced over the soggy ground. Somehow she had to help put the fire out.

One of their horses bounded out of the barn. Galloping, it nearly ran her down. She leaped out of the way and fell hard. Another thunderbolt hit a tall elm nearby. Brilliant white light flashed, followed by a deafening thunderclap. She covered her eyes, as well as her ears. The ground beneath her shook.

When she could, she looked up. In the open barn doorway, Joseph was waving both arms, beckoning her. She dragged herself up from the ground. Slipping on the wet grass, she hurried toward him. With the lightning flashing, she didn't need a lantern to see what had upset her father-in-law. Mary Dyke's son lay on the dirt floor of their barn.

"What happened to him?" she called over the continuing thunder.

"I don't know!" Joseph shouted back at her.

Matthew yelled, "I think he climbed the ladder in the hayloft and opened the door so the rain could douse the fire."

Verity looked up and saw that the fire was out. "What's he doing here? In our barn?"

"Don't know," Matthew said, "Joseph, help me get him into the house."

Within minutes, Matthew laid the boy on the kitchen table. Verity asked Joseph to check on and reassure Beth so she could examine Alec. Verity listened to his heart and felt for a fever. No fever. But the boy had a black eye, bruises and a split lip. Had he been fighting? Why was he hiding in their barn? Sodden and chilled from her own wet clothing, she tried to rouse him but had no luck.

The thunder still boomed outside, but it was more distant now. "The boy worries me." She looked toward Matthew and gasped. His hand was pressed against his forehead, blood flowing between his fingers. "Thee is hurt. What hurt thee?"

"Blasted horse knocked the stall door into me on his way out. Don't worry about me."

Wasn't that just like a man? Blood pouring from his head, but don't worry about him. Her exasperation moved her past her fear of the storm. She moved quickly to the pantry and collected her nursing equipment, a wash basin, a fresh towel and soap. "Sit." She pointed to the chair.

Grumbling, Matthew sat. She lit an oil lamp on the table and leaned close to him, examining the gash.

"This will need a stitch or two. I've got some experience nursing. I'll take care of it."

"Just clean it and use some sticking plaster to close it."

Ignoring him, she gently washed away the blood. It felt odd to be touching a man. His wet hair released the distinctive scent that was Matthew Ritter. She forced herself to focus on the gash on Matthew's forehead. He sat very still, probably as uncomfortable with this nearness and touching as she was.

Finally she was able to turn away, drawing in a ragged breath. She'd nursed other men without this breathless reaction. Matthew should be no different. She emptied the basin out the back door and returned the medical supplies to the pantry.

The chair behind her scraped as Matthew rose. "What are we going to do about Mary's boy?"

She looked out at the pouring rain. "This is not a night to go afield. We should get him out of his wet clothing and into a warm bed."

Matthew swung the thin boy up into his arms and carried him upstairs. Hearing the creak of the rocker in her room and realizing Joseph was rocking Beth, she directed Matthew to lay the boy down on Beth's empty white-canopied bed. Beth and Verity could share a bed as long as Alex needed to stay.

Verity gathered a clean nightshirt from Joseph's room and brought it back to Matthew. "Here, put this on him. It will be too big, but it will be dry." A pile of soaked clothes sat on the floor.

Matthew had lit the bedside candle and stood, looking down at the boy. His expression caught Verity's attention. "What's wrong?

Matt hesitated and then folded back the top edge of the blanket covering the boy. Verity gasped.

Chapter Four

The boy was covered in harsh purpling bruises—
hardly a spot of skin had been spared. Matt felt a wave
of anger wash over him.

The widow turned away, shuddering as if fighting
for control. "That couldn't have happened to him just
from the storm," she finally said in a low voice laced
with revulsion.

Matt had to stop himself from putting an arm
around her. No woman should have to see something
as cruel as this. "No, but it explains what he was doing
in our barn." Matt's low words scraped his throat. "He
was hiding. This isn't a normal whipping of a boy.
Somebody has beaten the living daylights out of him.
Somebody bigger and stronger." Anger steamed
through Matt. He had no doubt who'd done this. He
met the widow's eyes across the bed. But he couldn't,

wouldn't tell her who he thought was responsible. *Poor Mary. I have to think what to do to help, not make matters worse. But what? If I confront Orrin, he'll just beat the boy worse or turn on Mary.*

"What are we going to do?" Verity asked, echoing his thoughts.

"Let me think." This was a sticky circumstance. Going over to Orrin Dyke's house and beating the thug into the mud wouldn't help Mary or her son. But Matt had to fight himself to keep from doing just that. Dyke was lucky enough to have a son, and he treated him like this?

Matt glanced up at the rustling of the bedsheets. The widow was very gently and thoroughly checking each of the boy's limbs for movement. The candle cast her face in shadow. And for once, she was without her armor, her widow's weeds and tight corseting. In her muslin wrapper and slippers, she looked slender and almost frail. Very feminine.

This reaction rolled through him like the thunder in the distance. He throttled it and asked harshly, "Are any bones broken?"

"His legs, arms and shoulders move in the normal ways. But I'm sure that he has bruised or cracked ribs. Is there a doctor nearby?"

Her compassion touched him. He fought against showing this. "Not near. About eight miles from here. Do you think he is in need of a doctor?"

"I don't know. I can't get him to wake up. See here." She brushed back the boy's bangs and showed him an especially nasty bruise. She had long slender fingers and her hands showed signs of honest work.

For a moment the woman looked down, a soft expression on her face as she stroked the boy's cheek. Matt felt her phantom touch on his own cheek. He was conscious of both the sound of steady rain against the window and of the scent of lavender wafting from the woman. He dragged his gaze from her, forcing himself to study his surroundings. This must be her daughter's room. Pinafores hung on pegs by the door and a canopy covered the bed—it was a homey place that contrasted with the ravaged boy.

She reached across the bed and gripped his damp sleeve. "What can we do about this?" she whispered.

He shook his head and then, unable to stop himself, he laid his hand over hers.

A moan startled him. She released Matt's sleeve, breaking their connection. "Mama." The boy was waking.

"Alec, it's Verity Hardy."

The boy tried to sit up and groaned. The sound spoke of such deep pain that Matt found himself gritting his teeth.

"Don't try to sit up yet," she cautioned. "You're hurt."

Alec still struggled, trying to get up as the widow tried gently to hold him back.

Matt leaned forward. "Alec, I'm Matt Ritter, an old friend of your mother's. Lie back down. It's all right." He carefully pressed boy back down.

The boy looked up wide-eyed in the candlelight. "You're that Yankee. What happened? Why am I here?" Before Matt could answer, he saw fear flash in the boy's eyes. "I shouldn't be here." Again the boy thrashed feebly under the blanket, trying to get up.

"Alec, you must lie still." The widow held his shoulders down. "Mind me now."

At her quiet but insistent words, the struggle went out of the boy. He went limp. "What's happening, ma'am?"

"Thee helped us keep our barn from burning down," Verity answered. "Thee must have been hit in the head somehow. I couldn't wake thee. So we brought thee into the house."

"Ma'am, I should be getting home."

"No, I think it would be best if thee stayed the rest of the night here."

"But, ma'am, my mother needs me. Please."

Alec's words struck Matt like a blow to his breastbone. Was Orrin beating Mary right now? The urge to run to her rescue made Matt's heart gallop. He added his hand on the boy's shoulder over one of the widow's. "All will be well. You'll go home in the morning."

Panic widened the boy's eyes. "But my father—"

The widow touched the boy's fair wet hair. "Thee must lie back and rest. Trust us."

The boy appeared to want to argue, but fatigue and weakness overcame him. He whispered something that Matt could not understand and then his eyes closed again.

The widow touched the boy's forehead. Then she looked over at Matt.

When their eyes connected, he saw deep concern. Suddenly he felt his solitary bachelor state as he never had before. He looked away. "I think he'll sleep the rest of the night." He turned toward the door, wanting to put distance between them.

"Matthew Ritter," she asked again, "what can we do for this child?"

Her soft voice beckoned him to remain. "I'll think of something," he rumbled. He left her, his mind churning as he thought of Alec. And of how much longer he'd have to wait for the telegram that would whisk this woman— so dangerous to his peace of mind—out of his life.

Matt and the widow and her family stared at the telegram sitting open on the breakfast table. A military courier stationed at the railroad and telegraph depot had brought it just as they were sitting down to breakfast.

The telegram had been short and to the point. "Mrs. Hardy stay and start school wherever possible STOP Ritter move forward with school construction STOP Signed, The Freedman's Bureau." Matt had wanted to say STOP himself and had tried to hide his irritation, but he didn't think he'd done a very good job. The widow had merely read it aloud and then made no comment. Clearly she wasn't a gloater.

Then he thought to ask about Alec. "Is our visitor staying for breakfast?" The telegram had made him forget momentarily that there were more important things to deal with. His will hardened. An honorable man couldn't just ignore what had been done to the young boy—he had to act today.

The widow looked strained, glancing sideways at her little girl. "Our visitor left before I was able to invite him to stay for breakfast."

Beth glanced up at her mother with obvious curiosity. "We had a guest?"

"Alec stopped by for a bit, but he had to get home."

"Oh," Beth said, sounding disappointed.

Matt didn't like that Alec had left. Would he suffer for running away?

"I was wondering, Matthew, if we should drop by and visit Alec's parents." The widow gave him a pointed look.

"I don't think that's something we should do," he replied, aware that she didn't want her daughter to know of Alec's situation. Orrin would lash back unless the right person spoke to him. Men like Orrin only listened to those they dared not disregard, those they feared. And there was only one man in Fiddlers Grove Orrin might fear.

"But something should be…" Her voice faltered.

"Perhaps we should talk about this later," Matt said, nodding toward her daughter.

"Yes, we'll discuss it later."

Beth looked at both of them and then went back to eating her oatmeal.

Matt cleared his throat. "The surveyor will be here this morning to survey the school site before we start building, so I'll be busy with that today. Have you had a chance to hire us a housekeeper?"

"I will attend to that today," the widow replied, offering him a second helping of biscuits.

It was hard to stay annoyed that Mrs. Hardy was remaining. She brewed good coffee and made biscuits as light as goose down. He might as well just get over the aggravation of having someone—this woman—working with him. *We're here for the duration.* He forced a smile. "Good biscuits, ma'am."

She smiled her thanks and offered him the jar of strawberry jam.

He took it and decided not to hold the excellent jam against her, either. She couldn't help it if she was a good cook. All in all, it could have been worse. She wasn't much for nagging. He'd just go about building the school and signing men up for the Union League of America, and she'd start teaching school. They need meet only for meals.

He let the golden butter melt on the biscuit and blend

with the sweet jam, and inhaled their combined fragrance. Army rations weren't even food compared with what Mrs. Hardy put on a table. He hoped she was as good at hiring a housekeeper as she was at cooking.

He wondered briefly where she was supposed to start the school in Fiddlers Grove. Did the Freedman's Bureau think the locals would rent her space? *Not a chance.* Well, that was her job. He had enough on his plate, starting with Alec and Mary. His conscience wouldn't let him pass by on the other side of the road.

After breakfast, the widow sent her daughter out to feed the chickens and give the leftovers to the barn cats, who, along with the horses and the barn, had survived the night's storm. Joseph rose from his place at the table and asked without preamble, "What was wrong with the boy?"

"He had been beaten unmercifully," the widow replied.

Matt heard the mix of concern and indignation in her voice. His nerves tightened another notch.

"Disciplining a boy is one thing. Beating him is another." Joseph looked concerned, his bushy white brows drawing together. "Alec is a good boy, too."

"I don't know what to do. I've never dealt with anything like this." The widow lowered her eyes and pleated the red-and-white-checked tablecloth between her fingers.

Matt wished he could save her from worrying over this. "What can anyone do? A father has control over his children, absolute jurisdiction." The bitter words echoed Matt's frustration over his inability to take direct action. The world was the way it was and good intentions never went far enough.

Matt had decided he wouldn't tell the widow or Joseph what he planned to do. He didn't want to give her hope when there probably wasn't any. He had to admit to himself that he also didn't want her to know he'd tried and failed. He ground his molars, irritated.

"I will pray about this," the widow said. "All things are possible with God."

Matt gritted his teeth tighter. Prayer didn't help. He'd learned that while watching the life leak out of friends on the battlefield. He'd been the one who closed their eyes in death. Either God didn't hear prayers in the midst of cannon fire or Matt didn't rate much with God.

Knowing his opinion would shock the Quaker, he pushed up from his place. "I've got things to do. See about hiring that housekeeper and find a laundress. I think you'll find a lot of former slaves who will be happy to get work." He regretted sounding so brusque. But he couldn't help it. He was a captain—he was used to giving orders.

"Thank thee, Matthew."

Joseph gave him an approving look. "You show

you understand how much work it takes to run a household. You must have had good parents."

Uneasy, Matt looked at the older man, wondering where this comment had come from. "Yes, I had good parents."

Joseph nodded and walked outside, whistling. Matt hurried out after him, not wanting any more discussion about Alec. He'd deal with the surveyor and then he'd do what he'd known he must do sooner or later. Deathbed promises were a burden he couldn't ignore. And Alec could not be ignored.

Verity had left Beth at home with Joseph because, once again, she didn't know what kind of reception she'd receive. And she didn't want Beth troubled. Verity had a formidable errand this morning and could only hope that she was following God's prompting.

The memory of the battered young boy from last night haunted Verity. She had tried to turn Alec over to God, but the image of his injured body lingered in her mind. Some images were like that.

She had seen many sights during the war that she wished she could erase from her mind. But that wasn't possible. She wondered what images Matthew carried with him day after day, after four years of soldiering. What a burden. No wonder he was brusque at times. *I will be more patient with him.*

Her steps slowing with her reluctance, she

walked around St. John's Church to the house behind it. Like all the other houses in Fiddlers Grove, the parsonage looked as if it had had no upkeep for a long time. White paint was peeling and green shingles needed replacing. She said a prayer for boldness to help conquer the uncertainty she was feeling, and walked up the steps. Then she lifted her suddenly unusually heavy arm to knock on the door. It was opened by a black girl of about thirteen in a faded blue dress with tight braids in rows around her head. "Good morning," Verity greeted her. "Is the vicar in?"

"Yes, ma'am." The young girl eyed her as if wanting to say something, but unsure if she should.

"May I see him, please?" Verity smiled, her lips freezing in place.

The girl stepped back and let her in. "Wait here, please, ma'am."

Verity waited just inside the front door.

Within short order, the pastor emerged from the back of the house. He looked shocked to see her in his house—just what she'd expected. In everyday clothing, he appeared shorter and slighter than he had in his white vestments. He was rail-thin, like most everyone else in town, with gray in his curly brown hair.

"Good morning," she said, greeting him brightly with false courage. "I was wondering if I could have a few moments to discuss something with you."

The man looked caught off guard and puzzled. "I…I don't know what we'd have to discuss."

She tried to speak with the boldness of the apostle Paul. "I have come with funds and the authority from the Bureau of Refugees, Freedman and Abandoned Lands to open a school in Fiddlers Grove."

He gaped at her.

"And I need thy help." Her frozen smile made it hard to speak.

"My help? I've read about that infernal bureau in the paper. I'm not helping them. Bunch of interfering…" He seemed at a loss for words to describe the Freedman's Bureau in front of a lady.

"I hope you will listen to what I have to say." She swallowed to wet her dry throat.

"You are mistaken, ma'am. We lost the war, but that does not mean that we want Yankees telling us how to live our lives and taking our land." He moved forward as if ready to show her the door.

"I beg thy pardon, but how is having a school in Fiddlers Grove telling thee how to live thy life?" she asked, holding her ground.

"If it doesn't affect me, then why discuss it with me?"

"Please let me at least explain what I propose. Does thee have an office where we might discuss this in private?" *I will not be afraid.*

Maybe her calm persuaded him or the Lord had prepared her way, but he nodded and showed her to a den off the parlor. He left the door open and waved her to a chair. He took a seat behind a fine old desk. "Please be brief. I am studying for my next sermon."

Verity nodded, drew in air and said, "I did not realize that there was no free school here. I was a schoolteacher for two years before I married. It grieves me to see children growing up without education."

He glanced at the clock on the mantel. "I, too, wish there could be a free school in town, but there wasn't one before the war and there won't be one now that everyone is in such difficult financial straits."

She pressed her quivering lips together, knowing that her next words would shock him. "I have come to set up a school to teach black children and adults. But I think that it would be wrong to set up a school for only black children when the white children have no school. Doesn't thee agree?"

He stared at her. "Are you saying that you could set up two schools?"

"No. Why not one school for children of both races?" She forced out the words she knew would provoke a reaction.

"You are out of your mind. This town would never accept a school that mixed black and white children."

Praying, she looked at his bookshelves for a few moments and then turned back to him. "I don't understand. Is the offer of free education something to be refused?"

"The kind of free education you are talking about is not even to be considered. If you build such a school, they will burn it down." He stared hard at her, underlining his point with a scowl.

Her face suddenly flamed with outrage. They were poor and defeated, but still rigidly committed to the past. She tried to use reason. "There is great want here. Wouldn't men welcome the work of building a school and the cash it would bring?"

"You're a Yankee. You don't understand Virginia. White men farm, but Negroes do the laboring. They are the carpenters, plasterers, coopers and bricklayers."

"Well, that will change. It must, because no longer can Negroes be told what to do. They will choose what they wish to work at. Just as thee did. The old South is gone. It died at Appomattox Courthouse. Slavery has ended. And nothing will ever be the same here again." The truth rolled through her, smoothing her nerves.

He stared at her, aghast.

Now that she'd said what she'd come to say, she felt calm and in control. "It may be of no comfort to thee, but the North has changed, too. No people can go through the four years that we've been through, suffered through, and be the same on the other side. Doesn't thee see that?

"A school would be good for the whole town," she continued. "Why not let progress come? Why not let me rent thy church to use as a school until the new school is built? And the Freedman's Bureau may pay thy church rent, money that I'm sure thy church could use. Why not leave bitterness behind and be a part of a brighter future?"

After the surveyor had finished, Matt made himself head to the Ransford plantation to have the meeting he'd dreaded since he'd arrived. With imaginary crickets hopping in his stomach, he knocked on the imposing double door and waited for the butler to answer. When the door opened, he managed to say, "Good morning, Elijah." Looking into the familiar face yanked Matt back to his childhood.

"Did you wish to see the master of the house, sir?"

Even in his distraction, Matt noted the change from "the master" to "the master of the house." Matt appreciated Elijah's assertion of his freedom. He wondered again about Samuel. Did Elijah know where Samuel was? This wondering about Samuel chafed at Matt, but he couldn't speak of Samuel here and now. "Elijah, I need to speak to…Dace on a matter of importance—"

"Elijah, is that Matt Ritter?" Dace's gruff voice came from the nearby room.

"Yes, sir, it is."

"Bring him on back, please."

Elijah bowed and showed Matt into the small study

that Matt recognized as the room Dace's father had used for business. Memories flooded Matt's mind—coming in here and snitching toffees from the candy jar that still sat on the desk, the scent of his uncle's pipe tobacco.

After Elijah left them, Dace said, "I was wondering when you would come."

Matt sat down in the chair across the desk from his cousin, his only living blood relative, and looked him in the eye. Dace showed the telltale signs of war. He was gaunt, with deep grooves down either side of his face, and tired eyes.

"What brings you here?" Dace said over the rim of a coffee cup, sounding neither pleased nor displeased.

"Three matters, one from the past and two from the present. Which do you want to hear first?" Matt kept his tone neutral, too.

"Let's deal with the past first. I still like to do things in order."

This took Matt back to childhood also, to the many times he, Dace and Samuel had been planning on doing something daring like swim across the river at flood stage. It had always been Dace who planned out each test of their courage. "On her deathbed, my mother asked me to come back here and try to reconcile with you after the war."

"So that's why you came back?"

"Yes." *And with the foolish hope of coming home.*

But of course, Dace had never been forced to leave town, so he would not understand the feeling of not belonging anywhere or of having lost a home. Matt made sure none of this showed on his face. He would give Dace no chance to see that the events of their shared childhood still had the power to wound him.

"How do we reconcile? Shake hands? Remain on speaking terms?" Dace asked with a trace of mockery.

Matt's neck warmed under his collar. "I don't think real reconciliation can ever take place. There was hardly a chance before the war. Now there is even less hope."

"So why did you come?"

Matt's taut spine kept him sitting stiffly. "To fulfill my promise and to be a part of making the South change, even though it doesn't want to. That is the present matter I came to discuss."

"How will you make the South change? By force?"

"Force has already been used. My side won. Congress is moving forward, granting citizenship to former slaves and giving them the right to vote as citizens."

Dace just stared at him, tight-lipped.

"I'm hoping that it won't come to the point where I must ask for Union troops to put down opposition here. But I'm here to form a Union League of America chapter and to get a school built for former slaves and—"

The sounds of the front door slamming and rapid

footsteps alerted the men, and then Dace's wife rushed into the den. "Dace, you won't believe—" She broke off at the sight of Matt.

Matt rose, as did Dace. Of course, he remembered Lirit as a pretty girl, spoiled by her doting father on a nearby plantation. Though around the same age as the Quaker, Lirit looked older, somehow faded and thin and threadbare. "Hello, Lirit."

She drew nearer her husband as if Matt were unclean or dangerous. "Dacian, I'm sorry, I didn't realize that you weren't alone."

Matt ignored her obvious rejection. Lirit had never been one of his favorites, unlike Mary, whom he'd adored as a child. The thought of Mary started a fire in his gut. *Alec.* Where was he now and what had he suffered for running away and hiding?

"Matt and I were just discussing why he's come back to Fiddlers Grove," Dace said.

Lirit glanced at her husband. "You know that he's building a school for the children of former slaves?"

Dace nodded.

"Where did you hear that?" Matt demanded. He'd only told this to Mary, and he doubted Lirit and Mary were on speaking terms.

Lirit looked at him. "I was just at the parsonage. Your Mrs. Hardy had been there trying to talk the vicar into renting our church building as a school. She actually suggested that white children attend with black children."

Matt frowned. White children? "The school is to be only for black children and former slaves."

"The Quaker said that she didn't like to see the white children going without an education." Lirit's scathing tone made her opinion of this clear.

Matt began to leave the room. "I should go—"

"Wait," Dace said, stopping him. "You said you had come on three matters. We've only discussed two."

Matt sent a doubtful look toward Lirit.

Taking the hint, Dace touched his wife's shoulder. "May I have a private moment with Matt?"

"Certainly." Lirit walked out, haughtily pulling off her gloves. She snapped the pocket door shut behind her.

Matt and Dace stared at each other for a few heavy moments. "Last night our barn was hit by lightning. When we went to put out the fire, we found Alec Dyke unconscious and hiding in our barn. He'd been beaten mercilessly, and had bruises and cuts all over him. Were you aware that Orrin is probably abusing the boy?"

Dace looked worried and rubbed his chin. "I don't know what I can do about it."

"I know I can't do anything about it, but you might say something."

"It could just make matters worse."

"I hope you'll think this over, Dace. If anyone can stop Dyke, it would be you."

He turned to leave.

"Matt," Dace said, stopping him. "Where is the Quaker from, do you know?"

Matt thought this an odd question, but replied, "Pennsylvania."

Dace folded his hands in front of his mouth and stared out the window opposite him. "I don't like the idea of Yankees coming here and telling us how to live our lives. But it's like we are already in the coffin and they're tossing dirt on our heads and we don't even object."

Matt looked directly into Dace's eyes. "Change is inevitable." He didn't think he needed to say that even in the aftermath of the disastrous war, Ransford Manor was still the largest plantation for miles. And if Dace Ransford were in favor of something, people paused before they opposed it.

"Well, I've taken care of my obligation to my mother. The next time we meet, I'll just be the Yankee working for the Freedman's Bureau." Matt left without looking back, something he should have done fourteen years ago.

Chapter Five

In the autumn afternoon with golden leaves flutter-
ing above, Verity turned to see Matthew coming toward her on the road back to town. She waited for him
to catch up. Her mood lifted at the sight of him; after
all, Fiddlers Grove didn't abound with friendly faces.
And there was something so competent about him, so
focused. He was not a man who sought the easy path.
Or who would give up easily.

She knew he wished she had arrived after he'd left
Fiddlers Grove, but having him here was a great comfort to her. Of course, she wouldn't embarrass him by
saying that. The wind had ruffled his dark hair, giving
him a raffish look. She turned away so as not to betray
her reaction.

"What are you doing here?" he asked, breathing a
bit fast from his short sprint.

"I came here to hire our housekeeper. I asked Hannah if she could recommend someone and she said she could recommend herself." Verity smiled. She valued frankness in a world where people rarely told one another what they were really thinking. *Like this man.* She turned his own question back on him, asking, "What is thee here for?"

"Mrs. Ransford overheard you at the parsonage," he said, ignoring her question. "The whole town will know now what we're here for."

The wind had loosened the ribbons on her bonnet. Turning her back to the wind, she retied them tighter. "Was our work here to remain a secret?" *Like thy reasons for returning to a town that wouldn't welcome thee home?*

"What did you mean trying to rent the church for the school?" he scolded. "Surely you knew what the vicar's response would be."

"And what was his response?" she asked, a smile tugging at the corner of her mouth. Much better to be amused by his overbearing behavior than to take offense. Men always liked to think that only women gossiped, but men did it, too, as Matthew had just demonstrated. If he continued scolding her, she'd go ahead and ask about his cousin and this town. *It's not just nosiness, Lord. I need to know so I don't say things I shouldn't, assume things I shouldn't and cause trouble I could avoid.*

He scowled at her. "I'm sure it was not favorable."

From the corner of her eye she glimpsed movement behind her. She glanced over her shoulder and saw a stray dog following them. He looked like some kind of hound, with drooping ears, a long face with large brown eyes and a brown matted coat. The sight of his ribs almost pushing through his hide wrung her heart. *Poor creature.*

"No one is going to rent you space to teach in. I don't think you're really aware of the extent of anti-Yankee feelings here yet." A gust nearly took Matt's hat and he clamped it down with a frown.

She gave him a look and then turned around to the dog. She'd much rather help this poor animal than argue with Matthew Ritter. "Here, boy," she coaxed in a low voice. "Here, boy."

The animal stopped walking and sank to its belly, whimpering.

"What are you doing? Ignore the cur or he'll follow you home."

Ignoring his brisk order, she smiled. "That is my hope, yes."

He said something under his breath that sounded uncomplimentary about fool women.

She glanced up at him. "What was your rank in the army?"

"Captain. Why?"

Because thee still acts like a captain. But I didn't

enlist in the army. She chuckled to herself. Stooping, she smiled and cooed to the stray again, holding out her hand, palm up.

"What do you want a dog for?" he asked.

"Beth needs a friend. And since I am quite aware of the anti-Northerner bias here, I know she may not find a child who will befriend her. Strays always make the best pets." She crooned more loving words to the dog while Matthew huffed in displeasure. Men often behaved like this to cover a tender spot. Had Matthew had a dog when he was a boy? Or had that been denied him?

Matthew made a hasty gesture and the stray slunk behind a bush.

She rose, gave Matthew a pointed look and repeated, "What brought thee out here?"

"So Hannah is going to be our housekeeper?" He walked along beside her, ignoring her question as he ignored the stray.

I won't forget my question, Matthew Ritter. "Yes. I don't think that the Ransfords are paying them."

"Dace probably doesn't have anything to pay them with. It's funny—not really funny, but odd. Before the war, he had money and could have paid his people. Now he's supposed to pay them and he doesn't have any funds."

She quickened her pace to keep up with his longer strides. "It's an interesting twist, yes. Is that what thee discussed with thy cousin?"

"The surveyor staked out the site for the school. I can start hiring workers as soon as I get the wood and nails."

"I see." She decided her inquiries about his visit to his cousin didn't go far enough. *In for a penny, in for a pound.* "Why did thy family leave Fiddlers Grove?"

Matthew walked on, acting as if he hadn't heard her.

She glanced over her shoulder and saw that the stray dog was still warily following them. She paused and coaxed, "That's right, boy. Come home with us. I have a little girl who will love thee and then will love thee some more. And I have delicious leftovers that thee will enjoy." She decided to try Matthew once more. "Did thee visit thy cousin?"

He began whistling and kicking a rock along, completely ignoring her question.

So he must have, and the visit didn't prosper. Verity glanced back at the stray, still keeping up with them, and was touched by how dogs and humans both longed for family.

After supper, Verity and Beth sat on the back steps and watched the dog creep forward on his belly. Beth had put out a pan of leftover scraps and then retreated to the porch so that the dog would venture out to eat it. When he finished the scraps, she put out a pan of water between the porch and the flaming spirea bushes.

"Take a step back," Verity said in a low voice. Matthew had ignored the dog and gone to his cabin for the night. There was something in Matthew that needed healing, but she could see that he didn't want to admit that yet. The war had damaged them all. Why hadn't the South just given the slaves their freedom? Slavery had never made sense to her. Why had so many thousands had to die to end it? Why had her husband had to die? And why did thinking of Roger still hurt so?

Beth obeyed, stepping back and waiting. The dog snuffled the ground, crept over to the bowl of water and began to lap it—still with one wary eye watching Beth and Verity.

"I'm going to call him Barney," Beth confided.

"Oh, a very good name. He looks like a Barney." Verity squeezed her daughter's shoulder.

The beat of horses' hooves entering the yard scared the dog and he streaked into the bushes. A stranger dismounted and stepped up to her back porch. "Your servant, ma'am." He swept off his gray, worn Confederate officer's hat and bowed to her.

Verity recognized him then and a tingle of warning shot through her. He was Matthew's cousin, whom she had met at St. John's on Sunday.

"Mama, the doggy ran away," Beth lamented, rising.

The gentleman bowed to her. "Ma'am."

"Dacian Ransford, how good to see thee." Swallowing with difficulty, Verity offered him her hand, which he shook briefly. Then she looked down at Beth. "Dacian and I will go into the kitchen, and then thee can coax the dog out again. Remember to speak softly, move slowly and offer him thy open hand to sniff. But don't hurry him. He's been a wanderer for a while and is afraid of being hurt."

"Yes, Mama." Beth knelt down near the water dish, watching the bushes.

"Please, Friend, won't thee come and sit?" Maybe he wouldn't want to come into her home. If whites didn't sit with blacks in Virginia, did ex-Confederates sit with Yankees?

He nodded and motioned for her to take the lead, his expression polite, even curious.

Sensing his watchfulness, she became wary. She walked into the kitchen and went to the stove, where a pot of water simmered. She forced herself to go on as if ex-Confederate officers often visited her. "May I offer thee a cup of tea?"

"That would be quite welcome, ma'am."

Verity motioned him toward the chair nearest the door. She felt his gaze on her as she made his tea. After a few awkward moments she handed him a cup and broke the silence. "And to what do I owe this visit?"

He held the cup up to his nose and sniffed it. "Real black and orange pekoe." His voice was almost reverent.

"Yes, I prefer it to Darjeeling." She put some oat-meal cookies on a plate and sat down across from him. Was he going to fence with her, as his cousin had done on their way home today?

"You are a lover of tea then, ma'am?"

She nodded and had no trouble believing that this man appreciated the finer things of life. After all, she'd seen his wife. But after four years of the Union blockade, the South only had items it could produce on its own. Now that the blockade had ended, Confederate money was worthless. *Why is thee here? What could thee possibly want from me?*

She took a sip, trying to ignore his intense concentration on her, though it sent a shiver down her spine. She could wait for him no longer. "Pardon me, but I do not think that thee came to discuss tea with me."

He chuckled. "One can always tell a Northerner. Always the direct approach."

"I am afraid that thee is correct." She held her cup high. "But I hope I have not been impolite."

"No, I think it best that I come to the point." He paused and sipped his tea. "I've heard about your plans to teach at the Freedman's school my cousin is planning to build here."

She nodded. Was this the real reason he'd come? It didn't seem to ring true. He continued to study her face.

"Ma'am, your goal may be laudatory, but I do not think you will meet with success. Not enough time has passed since the hostilities ended. Passions are still running high here."

She set down her cup and leaned back, considering him. Why not be bold? "And it is not easy bearing defeat."

He grinned ruefully at her. "The direct approach. Again."

"In one way I agree with thee, Dacian Ransford." She traced the rim of her cup with her index finger. "The times are unsettled. But it is in turbulent times that great change can be made. And great change is what the South needs." He started to speak, but she held up a hand, asking for his indulgence. "I don't know if thee realizes it but this war has changed the South and the North and the West. Or maybe it has shown how the world is changing," Verity continued in measured tones, folding her arms around her to ease the chill her own words gave her. "The East and the West Coasts are now linked by railroad. The Atlantic Ocean has been spanned by telegraph cable. The North abounds with factories, industry and all manner of inventions. Our lives on the farm are passing away." She stared at her tea.

He set down his cup. "That may be true, but what if many in the South do not want to change?"

She looked him in the eye. "Wasn't that the issue that this war settled?"

"Touché." He acknowledged the hit with a slight nod. "We must change. But I fear that there are many who will not." He continued to study her face.

"I am not taking the danger to myself lightly. But I must remind you that I am used to going against common prejudices. I am a Quaker—or I should say, I was a Quaker until I married. I belonged to and was raised by people who did not go along with whatever was popular at the time. We did not mind dressing and speaking and thinking differently. We even defied the law that said we must return runaway slaves to their masters. My family were abolitionists even before the American Revolution. I was an abolitionist before *Uncle Tom's Cabin* was published and the cause became popular."

He looked over the rim of his cup at her. "I can only repeat that the South is unready for such sweeping change."

"I told thee I did not expect to be welcomed here with open arms. But the change will come whether people want it or not. There will be a school in this town for black children and freed slaves. The Thirteenth Amendment has passed and former slaves are now freemen."

Dacian looked pained.

She continued, "The Fourteenth Amendment will give them citizenship and the right to vote. The North is absolutely committed to making sure that slaves were not set free only to be enslaved in some other form. If former slaves are citizens, they can vote and defend themselves."

"The South will never ratify the Fourteenth Amendment," he countered, his voice hardening, "and I am afraid that educating Negroes will meet with limited success. Most do not have the intelligence."

She shook her head, sorry to hear his words. "I am afraid that the two of us will always disagree upon that issue. I have known educated black men and women and they are equal to us in intellect. Black skin does not announce inferiority."

"I'm afraid that the two of us will always disagree upon that issue," he said, using her words. "But I do see that the Freedman's Bureau will have its way here. And I do thank you for thinking of the white children, but I doubt that any white parent would allow their child to go to such a school."

"I'm sorry to hear that." She liked the man's honest face and wished he would see things differently.

He nodded to himself as he rose, as if he had decided something. "I think that you have come with the finest intentions, but the South is not ready."

"Then I fear for the South." She rose also and folded her hands, looking up into his eyes earnestly. *Let him hear me, Lord.* "The North will not have lost thousands and thousands of lives to achieve nothing. If the South will not change willingly, the Radical Republicans will jam these changes down Southern throats. President Johnson, a Tennessean, has been able to hold off the inevitable for a time, but his protection will not last.

The Radical Republicans hold power in Congress and they will not hesitate to use it."

"I have never before discussed politics with a woman." He gave her a wry half smile. "But I do not doubt the correctness of your assessment. You see, ma'am, the war continues." He bowed to her and walked toward the door.

She followed him, sorry to see a good man so misguided. "I bid thee good evening then. Please know that whatever I do, I do because I want to help, not hurt."

The man halted. "I have no doubt that your motives are the best. But even the best motives can't bring about what you wish. Thank you for the tea." He spoke as a friend, a deeply concerned one.

And she wondered why. Why did he sound as if he knew her?

He studied her face for another moment and then shook her offered hand and donned his hat. He was out the door, on his horse and gone quickly.

As Verity stared after him, Joseph walked inside. "I didn't expect us to start getting visitors so soon. Does that mean you're making progress?"

"I'm not exactly sure." Verity turned over in her mind all she had learned not from words, but from all the other unspoken language. She felt that she had now met all the major players in the drama of which she was a part, except for Orrin Dyke. And she'd set events in motion by speaking to the vicar at St. John's.

But I came to set those events in motion. The people here might be reluctant, but God's work could not wait forever.

The next morning when Matt sat down at the kitchen table, his foul mood vanished instantly when Hannah set before him a bowl of pearly white grits with a small pond of yellow butter in the middle. Salivating, he helped himself generously and nearly smacked his lips. *Grits. Manna.* Matt savored their texture and taste on his tongue. He hadn't had grits since his mother had passed away. "Thank you, Hannah."

Hannah chuckled. "The boy been North too long."

"What's that?" Beth asked, looking at the bowl. At her mother's frown, she added, "Please, Aunt Hannah."

"That's grits and they're good. You'll like them." Hannah turned back to the stove. "Now you eat up, little girl. You won't have fun on an empty stomach."

"I'm going to get Barney to let me pet him again today," Beth announced as she helped herself to a small serving of grits.

"Who Barney?" Hannah asked, pouring more coffee around the table.

"It's the mongrel Mrs. Hardy let follow us home yesterday," Matt said, trying to sound disgruntled to tease the little girl.

"What's a mongrel?" Beth asked, eyeing Matt.

"It means we don't know who his ma and pa were,"

Joseph said. "I think he'll make a good watchdog after he gets used to us."

Matt tried to lose himself in the mundane conversation, but his plans for the day kept nudging him. The thought of them nearly took away his appetite—even for grits.

"Barney is going to be a good dog." Beth rocked in her chair. "He was scared of that man last night, but after the man rode away, Barney let me pet him."

"I saw that Dace was here last evening," Matt said, trying to sound uninterested. "What did he want?"

"Thy cousin came for a short visit," the widow said, glancing pointedly at her daughter.

Matt got the message. *I can wait.* He shoved all this aside and with great satisfaction took a second helping of grits. "So, young lady," he asked, "how do you like grits?"

"I haven't made up my mind yet, sir," Beth replied, stirring her spoon in her grits. "I like Aunt Hannah's scrambled eggs, though."

"Thank you, child." Hannah nodded toward Beth.

Matthew cleaned up his plate and rose. "Well, I've got a lot to do today." *A fool's errand and then probably a long ride.*

"Aunt Hannah, can I have the leftovers for Barney, please?" Beth asked. "And may I be excused, Mama?"

Hannah nodded. Verity smoothed her hand over the child's hair. "Yes. Stay in our yard."

Beth agreed and with pan of bacon ends and leftover eggs, she skipped out the door, calling, "Barney!"

"I think I'll sit on the front porch and whittle some and watch the leaves turning." Joseph thanked Hannah for breakfast.

Matt did the same, and the widow preceded him out the back door. They paused at the top of the steps to the yard. "What did my cousin come to see you for—if you don't mind my asking," Matt amended.

The morning sunlight glinted in her hair. He liked seeing her without her black bonnet. He imagined rubbing her springy curls between his thumb and forefinger. He clenched his hands, as if to ensure that they stayed put.

She rested one hand on the railing and blinked at the bright morning sunshine. "I don't mind telling thee, because it wasn't a personal visit. Thy cousin came to warn me away. He thinks the South isn't ready for change."

Anger burned in Matt's throat. He'd already told his cousin on no uncertain terms—

"Can thee think of any other reason he would come besides telling me not to expect the town to accept our school?"

"No, I can't." *I won't.*

She studied him as if trying to figure out if he were being frank.

That grated. But he'd been pretty unforthcoming

when they'd met on the road home from the Ransford place. She knew there were things he wasn't telling her.

Should he tell her, now that she was staying? He kept noticing little things about her. Now it was her dainty ivory ears and he shifted his gaze past her to the mutt noisily lapping water that Beth had just pumped for him. "I've got an errand to do. It's time I get busy getting building supplies and hiring men."

"I'll wish thee good day, then. I still have some curtains to hang." She went back inside.

As he walked toward town, he tried to picture himself telling Verity about his childhood with Dace and Samuel. A wave of guilt hit him as he thought of Hannah and Elijah—were they wondering why he had not asked them about their son, whom he had loved like a brother as a child?

He hadn't found the right moment, or at least that's what he'd been telling himself. But the truth was, he wasn't sure he wanted to know what happened to Samuel. He wasn't sure he could stand to hear it.

Soon Matt stepped into Hanley's store. He'd been in town for well over a week now and it was time to launch his attack. Silence fell upon the crowded gathering place of the village. Matt went directly to Hanley as if they were the only two in the store.

Hanley greeted him from behind the counter with a wary nod. "What can I do for you today?"

"I was wondering if you'd like to order some lumber and building supplies for me so I won't have to ride to Richmond." Matt thought that giving the local storekeeper the chance to make some money might help with popular opinion about the school.

He heard footsteps behind him as someone entered the store, but he didn't look back. "I also want to know if there are any carpenters in the area."

"Is this for that school of yours?" The voice came from behind Matt.

It was funny how after all these years, Matt still knew Orrin Dyke's belligerent and mocking voice. He turned slowly, feeling every eye on him. Matt stared at the big beefy man, who was a head taller than him. "Yes."

"I'll tell you straight to your face, then. We ran your family out of town once and we can do it again." Everyone in the store and outside on the bench had frozen into place. A heavy feeling of expectation expanded in the silence.

"No doubt I am not wanted here," Matt countered, his blood simmering at the mention of his family being forced out of town. "But I am going to stay long enough to build the school and prepare the former slaves to vote—"

With only a few strides, Orrin covered the distance between them. "Get out of town or you'll wish you had."

"Try anything and you'll end up in jail." *Where you belong.* Matt stared at Orrin's cruel face and thought of how his mother had cried as they drove out of town. And the recent memory of Alec's battered body bumped Matt's hostility up another notch. *Bully. Go ahead and try something. Give me a reason to—*

Orrin raised his fists. Matt moved into fighting stance, ready to defend himself, relishing the chance to release his anger on this very worthy target.

"Orrin," Hanley declared, "I have no quarrel with you. But I don't want any fighting in my store."

Orrin bristled. "I won't have any Yankee coming here and trying to give the coloreds uppity ideas. There will be no school for them in this town." He ended his statement with a crude epithet. The women and a few older men gasped at this public impropriety.

"There are ladies present," a very deep and completely unexpected voice chided from the doorway.

Just as Matt had instantly recognized Orrin's voice, he knew who'd spoken. He swung around to the entrance. "Samuel." And that was all he could say. It took all his strength not to hurry to Samuel and throw his arms around him. *Samuel. Friend.*

Wearing good clothes and a rifle on his shoulder, Samuel removed his hat and nodded. "Matt, it has been a long time."

Over fourteen years. Matt's throat constricted, but

he forced out the words, "Samuel, glad to see you." It was a completely insufficient response to Samuel's homecoming. But with half the town gawking at them, Matt didn't trust himself to say anything further.

Orrin spat out a stream of nasty curses. "You ain't welcome in town, either," he yelled at Samuel, his face and neck now a bright ugly red.

Samuel merely stared into Orrin's eyes as if daring him to do more than curse. He looked as if planting a fist in Orrin's nose would be pure pleasure.

The outraged white man swung away from Matt and charged Samuel.

Samuel casually slid the rifle on his shoulder into his hands and aimed it at Orrin.

Matt couldn't believe it. He'd not thought it possible for the tension in the room to increase, but it spiraled upward to a frightening pitch. A black man pointing a gun at a white man. All the men surged to their feet, ready to strike down this effrontery.

"There will be no pitched battle in my store!" Hanley barked. "Do you hear me? I won't have it!"

Orrin ignored him and snarled at Samuel, "You get out of town. If you come here for your ma and pa, get them and leave. Quick." Orrin shouldered past Samuel and stormed out the door.

Samuel lowered his rifle and completely ignored Orrin's parting words. "I was on my way through town to Ransford's when I saw you through the window,

Matt. How are my mother and father? Have you seen them?" he asked, as if nothing had happened.

Swallowing with difficulty, Matt could hardly keep hidden all the emotions dancing through him. "Your parents are fine. You will find Hannah at my place, the Barnesworth house. She just started as our house-keeper."

Samuel nodded his thanks. "What has brought you back to town, Matt?"

"I am here from the Freedman's Bureau to build a school. I am hiring carpenters and others in the build-ing trade."

"That is good news. I know how to swing a ham-mer. I don't know how long I'll be in town—I have unfinished business I need to take care of—but you can count on me for some work."

Matt offered Samuel his hand, to the shock of those in the store. Clearly they weren't ready to accept white and black men shaking hands yet. Well, they might as well start getting used to it.

"Are you headed home now?" Samuel asked.

"No, I have business here and perhaps in Richmond."

"I'll be off to visit my mother, then. I'll see you later, Matt." Samuel nodded politely and strolled out the door.

Matt acted as if he didn't notice the hostile glances sent his way. He turned back to the storekeeper. "Mr. Hanley, do you want my business or will I have to ride to Richmond?"

Chapter Six

That evening Matt found himself both eager and reluctant to go home. Riding home under the flaming red maples, he knew he'd have to face Samuel again. With Hannah at the Barnesworth house as housekeeper, Matt couldn't imagine the widow not opening wide the home to celebrate the return of Hannah's son. So he'd have to deal with Samuel's homecoming and in some way hold everything from the past deep inside. This predicament came, of course, as a result of coming back here. No wonder so many veterans were heading west. In one way, he wished he were halfway to Colorado right now.

In the hours since the confrontation at the store, Matt's memory had kept up a steady flow of memories of Samuel, only a year older than he. Matt recalled swimming in the creek on golden summer evenings, going rabbit hunting in crisp winter mornings with Sam—and Dace. Then a nervous deer peered out from the line of poplars along the road and darted in front of Matt, flaunting its white tail.

Holding his horse from shying, he had the same sensation of trying to hold back dozens of questions to ask Samuel. Where had he been? Why hadn't anyone spoken about him when Matt returned? These questions disturbed his already shaky equilibrium. They had been a threesome—Matt, Samuel and Dace. Seeing Samuel only pointed up that Dace was still lost to him, probably for good, forever. Why did that twist his insides?

No matter—Matt couldn't avoid going home. He cantered down the lane, nearing the Barnesworth house. Long before he saw the crowd around his back porch, he heard the jubilation—snatches of song and loud voices. He slowed his horse to a walk and approached the back porch.

"Good evening, Mr. Ritter," silver-haired Elijah greeted him.

Matt smiled and lifted his hat in hello. "You must be happy tonight. You have your son again."

"Yes, sir, I am praising the Lord for it. Now Hannah and I can be easy about him."

Matt wondered if Elijah would feel easy when he heard that his son had pointed a gun at Orrin Dyke today. And publicly offered to work on building the

Freedman's school. But it wasn't the place or time to address this. Matt turned his horse toward the barn.

"Good evening, Matthew," the widow greeted him as she stepped out the back door. She was carrying large pans of cornbread and a pot of butter toward the tables set up under the oaks. "You're just in time for Samuel's welcome-home meal."

What would she look like dressed in some color other than black? That bright copper hair clashed with the somber black. Pushing aside this nonsense, he touched the brim of his hat and headed toward the barn. He'd been right. The Quaker welcomed the celebration and insisted on hosting it.

This made him regret how unwelcoming he'd been the night she'd arrived. He took his time unsaddling and rubbing down his horse. He enjoyed the smell of horse and the routine, as well as the quiet of the barn, which contrasted with the jubilation so near.

But finally he had to go to the pump in the yard and wash his face and hands in the cold, bracing water. He headed for the long table under the oaks that had just begun to turn bronze. Verity had decimated their flock of chickens to provide for so many guests. The table was completely covered with bowls of sweet corn, greens, platters of cornbread and fried chicken.

He went to stand behind the empty chair at the head of the table. It gave him a funny feeling—he'd never taken this seat, the position his father had always occupied. But he was the man of this unusual household. Beaming, Verity stood to his right with Beth and Joseph and across from her were Samuel's family. Samuel was standing to Matt's left. Matt resisted the temptation to consider himself a part of these families. *I'm alone and I might as well accept it here and now.*

At Verity's quiet request, Elijah said a prayer of thanks for the return of his son and the food God had provided. And then Hannah sat down next to Samuel, taking her husband's hand as though drawing from him the power to do this—to sit at a table with white people.

This gave Matt the boost to begin asking the questions he'd wanted to ask. "Samuel, no one has told me how and when you left home."

"When I was fifteen, I ran away." Samuel helped himself to the bowl of sweet corn and passed it on. "I'd heard of an Underground Railroad stop that I thought I could get to before anyone discovered me missing. So I took off one spring night."

"Without telling his parents," Elijah added with a mix of pride and reproof.

"It must have been quite a shock for thee," the widow said.

Her soft voice reminded Matt of velvet. He looked down at his plate and wondered where his appetite had gone.

"It was a shock," Hannah said, and then pressed her lips together as if holding back tears.

Samuel looked sorry. "I know, it was hard of me. But I thought it best I just go, and I was young and heedless. All I wanted to do was get to freedom and I didn't care about anything else."

So Samuel had left two years after that awful night that had forced Matt's family to leave town. Matt noticed that the widow had stopped eating and was looking at Samuel as if trying to figure something out. Then it occurred to Matt—what had happened to make Samuel take the dangerous flight from slavery? What had happened to drive Samuel to care for nothing but freedom?

Matt listened as Samuel told about the Underground Railroad stop and traveling north by night with a "conductor." The table was quiet as everyone listened to Samuel, who now sounded more like a Northerner than a Virginian. And he had an aura of confidence, which Matt had noticed earlier as Samuel pointed his rifle at Orrin.

As if he'd read Matt's mind, Samuel said, "I've told my parents of our meeting at the store this morning, and about the school you're building."

Verity sat up straighter and sent Matt a questioning look. He avoided her gaze.

"Yes," Elijah joined in, "I think I can get you a few more hands. The Ransfords can't afford to pay their servants and field hands. The mas…" Elijah took a deep breath and corrected himself, "*Mr. Ransford* has tried to get everyone who hasn't left already or who has come back to sign work contracts. But he can't and won't pay until December after harvesting and selling the crop."

"How are times here, Matt?" Before Matt could reply, Samuel added, "I'll answer my own question. I have never seen this town look so bedraggled."

"Virginia bore a great deal of hardship throughout the war," Elijah said, nodding soberly.

"And don't I know it. So many battles were fought on this soil." Samuel cleared his throat and said with obvious pride, "I served in the Union Army."

Every slaveholder's worst fear had been realized when the Union Army had let free and runaway blacks enlist and fight. And Matt knew the black division had served bravely. Samuel should be proud. "So that's where you got your rifle."

Verity didn't look pleased at the mention of rifles.

"Yes, and I learned how to use it, too," Samuel said, a hint of iron in his voice.

Matt could not stop himself from adding, "Well, you'd better after you pointed it at Orrin Dyke." Hannah stopped eating and looked frightened, and Matt regretted what he'd said.

Samuel patted his mother's hand. "I was just letting

people know not to tread on me. Or mine. I've grown fangs."

Matt knew that he and Samuel were the only armed men standing against Orrin and his ilk. He was fairly certain that Samuel would have to do more than just point his rifle before that school was built.

"It must have been very hard for thee not knowing where thy son was all those years," Verity said, her voice laced with sympathy.

Matt realized that whatever this woman said, it always came from deep in her heart. A precarious way to live.

Hannah nodded, brushing away a tear. Elijah said, "After the war, we stayed here because we didn't want to make any changes until we located Samuel. And we had hopes that we might hear something from or about Abby." Elijah looked at his son.

Abby? Matt hadn't thought of her for years. A pretty girl, she was the daughter of the Ransfords' blacksmith. Samuel had already been sweet on Abby at thirteen. What had happened to Abby?

The widow looked inquiringly at Samuel, but Elijah answered, "Abby was the girl Samuel wanted to marry."

Hannah spoke up for the first time, as if forcing herself to say words she hated. "During the war, she was sold. A slaver came through buying slaves, we think, to take to Mississippi."

"But Abby might have been sold anywhere between here and Mississippi," Elijah added. The table had gone very quiet and Samuel's expression had hardened. To Virginia slaves, Mississippi had been synonymous with hell. The slaves had feared being "sold South" more than anything else because with no way to visit or send word, it tore apart their families forever.

"I'm sorry to hear that," Matt replied. But even though he knew right where Dace was, his family had been broken forever.

"Matt, I'll try to help you get the school built," Samuel said, "but I plan on going South to find Abby."

Hannah drew a deep breath. "Miss Verity, we thank you for sending the letter trying to find our son. We didn't know that he was already on his way here."

"I'm very happy that thy son has returned." Verity smiled. "And I will add Abby to my prayers. I'd like to make an announcement to all of you," she said, raising her voice. "I will be starting the school on my front porch on Second day morning next. I hope everyone will send their children seven to twelve years old to register and begin learning to read. Any adults who would like to learn can register when we've got our school built."

There was a moment of silence and then a burst of excited chatter. Matt frowned, but what could he say? The Quaker was in charge of teaching and he had a school to build. Then Matt recalled Orrin Dyke's red angry face. Well, what would come would come.

* * *

The sound of breaking glass woke Verity. She leaped out of bed, pulled on her wrapper and stood in the hallway, listening. She could hear Joseph's soft reassuring snores. She peeked into her daughter's bedroom—Beth was sleeping the slumber of the innocent. Had she imagined the glass breaking in a dream? What should she do if—

She heard the back door downstairs open and shut. Heart pounding, she hurried down the steps and into the kitchen. There in the moonlight stood Matthew, looking as if he'd just dragged on clothing and run here. She fought the pull to go to him. Again he had his rifle in hand.

"I heard glass breaking," she whispered, trying not to look at him.

"Me, too." As he moved to the window, his footsteps crunched on shards of glass. He pushed back the white curtain with the barrel of his gun and looked out.

She stood there, still trying to make sense of being awakened. "Was it a bird hitting the window?"

"No." He turned to her holding a rock in his hand. A large rock.

Verity gripped the back of the nearest kitchen chair. Rocks didn't fly through windows on their own. "I'll get the broom." At the sound of more breaking glass, she whirled around.

With the butt of his rifle, Matthew broke the remaining glass in the window and brushed all the glass to the floor.

Verity stifled a cry. "Would thee light the lamp or a candle? I don't want to miss any of the glass in the dark. And I'm barefoot."

"I don't know if that's wise," Matt said, his voice low. "A light will show our silhouettes and I don't want us to be targets."

"Targets?" She pressed a hand over her thumping heart.

"Yes, the rock thrower might still be out there." He laid his rifle down on the table and took the broom from her.

"Did thee see anyone on thy way in?"

He urged her into the closest chair and then began sweeping up the glass. "No, but that doesn't mean someone isn't still out there."

"I see." In the low light she watched him sweeping, her bare feet perched on the ladder-back chair rung.

"A rock's not such a big deal, you know," he said gruffly.

She curled her toes under. Oddly, being barefoot made her feel more vulnerable. "I know thee is trying to reassure me, but that only leads me to ask, what does thee consider a big deal?"

He didn't reply.

She couldn't see his eyes well enough to get a sense

of what he was truly thinking, feeling, hiding from her. "I see thee has brought thy gun into the house," she said as he emptied the dustpan of shattered and clinking glass into the bin just inside the pantry door. "Perhaps we should discuss what thee truly thinks the town's response to our school will be and make plans in case violence is used against us." She tried to keep her voice even, but it trembled on the final syllable, giving her away.

Matt's jaw tightened. The Freedman's Bureau ought to have known better than to send a woman with a child into hostile territory. Just because Lee had surrendered didn't mean that Virginia had.

"I'll make us tea." The widow tried to rise.

He stopped her. "You should go back to bed." *I do not want to talk about what we may be heading into.*

"No, we need to discuss this. Thee has made thyself very clear that thee expects us to be on the receiving end of…" Her voice faltered.

"Receiving end of nastiness," he finished for her. He went to the stove and lit it, setting the kettle on the burner. Maybe a cup of tea would settle her nerves and he could get her to go upstairs more quickly.

"Didn't I warn you the night you arrived that you should turn around and go home?" he asked, feeling some savage pleasure at saying this. He sat down near her.

"It was a rock, not a cannonball. I will not be afraid. God's work cannot wait just because of a few—"

"How do you know it's just a few?" Maybe it was because she was a civilian that she couldn't conceive of someone wanting to harm her. He'd had four years of Confederates aiming gun and cannon at him to blow him away. And he'd seen the lethal hatred in Orrin Dyke's eyes.

In the moonlight she stared at him. "I know thee doesn't want me here."

"It's not that," he said, feeling heat rise in his face. He was getting too used to this woman's daily presence, to her direct way of speaking in her velvet voice and the way her face dimpled when she smiled. "I don't want you to get hurt." His words felt as if they'd come from deep inside. Silence. He hadn't meant to say that.

"And I don't want thee to get hurt, either, Matthew."

Her softly spoken words burst through him like a summer sun.

She went on, "Let's not waste any more words on this. I'm employed by the Freedman's Bureau, just like thee. I've been told to continue with my teaching and I'm going to. We must work together." She laid her hand over his.

His reaction was instant. Without meaning to, he turned his hand up and grasped her hand in his. Her palm was callused but her small hand was soft. It had been so long since he'd touched a woman's hand like this, alone in the shadows. More than just a gloved-hand clasp. More—

The kettle whistled and he rose, pulling his hand from hers. Soon he was setting a steaming cup before her.

She lifted her cup and inhaled. "I keep hoping that the people here will see that there's a better way."

He snorted and sat again. "They are blind. For some reason, they cling to slavery even when it has been abolished and even when it cost them countless lives and everything else. It makes no sense."

"It does in a way."

"I don't see it."

"The farther one lives away from the truth, the deeper the darkness one lives in. Jesus is the light of the world. If thee doesn't have Him, thee lives thy life stumbling around in the darkness of sin."

I know about darkness, Matt thought to himself.

"I like Samuel," Verity said.

He looked at her in the faint natural light. He smiled, her steadfast commitment to hope and compassion lifting his gloomy perspective. "I do, too."

"Thee and I have been put together and must work together. Please, Matthew, don't worry about me. That is not thy job here. God has provided angels to watch over us." She rested her hand on his again. "Now, what does thee think we will be facing in the weeks to come? Tell me honestly."

No matter what she said, protecting her was his job. No honorable man could do differently. He sipped his tea, but didn't move his other hand, not wanting to break their connection, even though he knew he should.

He watched the moving shadow of branches on the wall. "I think that we'll have to expect vandalism at the building site, at the very least. Once the school is begun, you should not go into town without me or Joseph with you. Or be here alone."

"Thee thinks then that I might be physically attacked."

The woman was cool, he'd give her that. She sounded as if they were merely discussing an interesting matter in the newspaper. "Yes, I think that is a very real possibility." He wanted to clasp her hand tighter, but worried she'd pull away if he did. What was happening? They shouldn't be sitting here, their hands touching. They were colleagues, but that was an odd situation, too. How often did a man and woman—not married to each other—work together?

She nodded. "I will do as thee says."

His eyes widened at this and he snorted again.

She chuckled softly. "I can listen to reason, Matthew. But still, I will be praying there will not be such opposition. I still hope that God may soften the hearts here and that His light will shine in this present darkness. I will keep thee apprised of my movements and try not to expose my child or myself to needless danger. But we must not make a rock into a cannonball in our minds. If God be for us, who can stand against us?"

Matt's mouth twisted down, but he hid it behind the cup. *Against us? Only most of Fiddlers Grove, including my own blood.* She drew away her hand and he was suddenly cold.

A week later, Verity prepared to greet her new pupils on her front porch. The day was cool—autumn was stealing over Virginia. She had set up a desk and had a stack of slates, a box of chalk and a fresh ledger to enroll her students. She smiled. "Good morning, students."

In the distance she heard the rumble of men's voices. Yesterday Matthew had hired several former slaves with carpentry experience. Today they were unloading the wood that had arrived from Richmond this morning. *Well, Lord, we're beginning our school today. Help me to start on the right foot. And please protect us.*

The children on the porch dressed in worn clothing were very leery of her and her stomach fluttered. Would someone try to stop her today? She cleared her thick throat.

"I want the boys to move to the left side of the porch, and the girls to move to the right side." No child moved until Beth did, and then the children obeyed her instructions with a bit of mumbling and giggling.

"Every morning I expect you to come to school on time and sit on the correct side of the porch or room—"

"But we ain't got any chairs," one little boy pointed out.

"Then thee will sit on the floor," Verity said, catching movement from the corner of her eye. She tried to see what or who had moved within her peripheral vision.

"Ain't a school supposed to have chairs?" the same little boy asked.

"Be quiet, you," one of the girls hissed. "Ma told us to be good and not sass the teacher. I'm tellin' if you don't stop—"

The boy stuck out his tongue at her. "Tattletale—"

"That's enough," Verity said in her most authoritative voice. Perhaps she had just imagined the movement—she gave up trying to find the source. "I am now going to enter thy names in the ledger." The children began telling her their names all at the same time. "No one is to speak unless I give them permission. Thee must raise thy hand and, if I give permission, then thee may speak." At the sight of a boy shoving another, she added, "And if anyone touches or hits someone else, they will be punished."

These words silenced and petrified the children. Verity walked to the desk and seated herself behind it, dipped her pen in ink and said, "We will begin with the boys. First boy, step up here please and state thy name." The first boy didn't move until he was shoved from behind and then he approached her with lowered eyes.

"Your name, please?"

"I'm Thaddeus." He set one bare foot on the other.

The same girl hissed, "You suppose to say, 'ma'am'."

"Ma'am," Thaddeus added.

Verity carefully wrote his name down. "What is thy surname?"

The little boy looked at her in some confusion. "I don't got one of those…ma'am."

"What is your father's name?" Again, something barely moved at the edge of her vision.

"Josiah, ma'am."

"Since he has been freed, has he added a second name to that?"

"I guess it's Ransford. He used to belong to Mr. Ransford. But my mama, she lived on the Ellington plantation."

"Then thee is Thaddeus Ellington Ransford." Verity finished writing his name while trying to glimpse who was moving in the surrounding oaks. The raised voices of the men who were now sawing wood floated over to the makeshift school.

When she looked up she found the little boy beaming at her. "Thank you, ma'am, I like that name. It's big."

"Then thee will have to live up to thy name, won't thee?" Verity smiled at Thaddeus. "Now please go and sit at the end of the line."

Thaddeus puffed up his chest and strutted to the rear of the line to sit down. After Thaddeus's example, each child presented himself and gave his name and who his parents had belonged to. They were thrilled when each of them was given a new "big" name.

Verity had nearly finished enrolling students when the talkative little girl, Sassy Ellington Ransford, hailed her. "Ma'am, ma'am, why is that white boy sittin' in the tree watchin' us? Can he do that?"

Verity looked where the girl was pointing and glimpsed fair hair amidst the oak leaves. So that's what she'd been seeing—Alec. Was he spying on her or the men building the school? Or did he just want to learn? Verity looked at Sassy. "There is no law against sitting in a tree. Now we will begin to learn the alphabet. At first I will teach you to say the sounds in order and then we will begin learning to write each one."

"What's an alphabet?" Thaddeus asked out of turn.

"What did I say about raising thy hand and waiting for permission to speak?" Verity was secretly enjoying the freshness of her eager students, but she had to instill the discipline that was so important to learning.

Thaddeus's hand shot into the air. After her nod, he asked, "What's an alphabet…ma'am?" He cast a triumphant look at his sister.

"The alphabet is the basis of written language. Each

letter represents or stands for a sound. In order to read, one learns the letter for each sound."

Another boy raised his hand.

Verity nodded. "Yes?"

"Are you going to teach us Latin?"

"Latin? Why would thee need to learn Latin?" she asked in surprise.

"'Cause edjicated people knows Latin. I come to get edjicated."

Verity hid a smile. "One must learn English first. Latin comes later."

"Are you certain sure?" Sassy asked, and then covered her mouth with her hand. "Sorry, ma'am."

Verity nodded and then unfolded a large piece of heavy cardboard on which she'd printed the letters of the alphabet. She sensed movement in the oak tree again. A gust of wind shivered the oak leaves and she saw that it was indeed Alec, leaning forward to see her chart. How sad to have to sit in a tree to learn.

In the distance, she heard Matthew's voice giving directions and she paused to listen. For a brief moment, everything felt perfect. *Father, bless the building of this school and these students. Bring healing to Fiddlers Grove. Please.*

Then she recalled the sounds of breaking glass in the night. Would a rock through their kitchen window be the end of opposition?

Chapter Seven

During the quiet after supper, Verity walked outside in the twilight to Matthew's cabin. She needed to discuss something with him. In the still green yard, Beth was playing catch with Barney. As Verity passed her daughter, Beth announced with beaming pride, "Mama! Look! Barney brings the stick back to me every time!"

"Wonderful!" Verity waved, continuing on her way over the uneven ground. By now the grass would be turning brown in Pennsylvania and her father and brothers-in-law would have harvested the crops. Here there was just a nip of autumn in the air this evening. Rubbing her arms to warm them, she wished she'd donned her lamb's-wool shawl. She wouldn't be able to hold class on the porch much longer. Fall and winter came later in Virginia than Pennsylvania, but they were coming. Virginia was not so far south that they wouldn't get a hard freeze and perhaps some snow for Christmas.

The thought of Christmas pricked her heart. It would be her first Christmas away from her large family. Though they'd never celebrated the day with a tree, they'd always taken off from work and had a festive meal and small gifts. And Verity had enjoyed the pine boughs, wreaths, mistletoe and red ribbons her neighbors had decorated their houses with. She was knitting a special present for Beth this year, hoping it would ease the pain of being so far away from six doting aunts.

Another thought tugged at her heart. Matthew had family here but his remained a family divided. The wind was loosing her hair from its bun—as it always did. She shoved her hairpins in tighter. She wished she could help Matthew and free him from the dark shadows of the past he still carried. Like most men, Matthew did not even admit to emotions.

But she was not fooled. He must have come here to reconcile with his cousin. Maybe that's why he hadn't answered her questions about Dacian that day they'd walked home together from the Ransford plantation. This heavy thought weighed upon her, slowing her steps. It was odd how feelings could affect her physically. How could an emotion actually tug at her?

She arrived at the small cabin near the barn. The door was ajar, so she called, "Matthew, may I come in?"

He appeared at the door. "What's wrong?"

The assumption that she sought his aid had become his usual response. She gave him a half smile. "I need to discuss something with thee, something I didn't want Beth to hear. May I come in?"

His reluctance to allow her access to his sanctuary showed plainly on his face, but good manners dictated he must give way to a lady. He stepped back. "Of course."

She entered the cabin. His rifle stood at the ready next to the door. A rope bed covered with a worn army blanket was tucked against the wall. A candle burned on a small round table with two straight-back chairs. A soldier's room. An open journal lay upon the table with a steel-pointed pen and inkwell beside it. That interested her. Matthew kept a journal.

"What did you want to discuss?" he asked, sounding uncomfortable.

She pulled out the chair nearest her, unused to Matthew's private territory, and primly sat down. Matthew took his place beside the journal, which he moved aside. Evidently the ink was still wet, because he didn't close it. She wondered if her name appeared on its pages and then forced her mind back to the matter at hand.

She drank in the comfort of his nearness in this still strange place and then drew in a deep breath. "Alec sat in one of our oak trees all through school today."

"And?" he asked.

She pursed her lips. "I can't decide if he was there out of curiosity. Or out of a desire to learn. Or because his father sent him to spy on us."

Matthew studied her and then began to tap the table with the little finger of his left hand.

She studied him in turn. There was a deeper meaning in their unspoken exchange. Matthew had become important in her life here. His keep-away veneer remained persistent, but she was beginning to penetrate, glimpse the true soul that was Matthew Ritter.

"Does it matter why Alec was there?"

"It does. We've done nothing about his situation."

"I told my cousin about the beating." He sounded as if this were one of the hardest things he'd had to do since arriving in Fiddlers Grove.

Matthew, I know it's hard for thee to talk about thy cousin. I'm sorry. "And what did Dacian Ransford suggest?"

"He said that talking to Orrin might cause the boy more harm than good." His deep voice made his words even graver.

She sighed. "I wish the world were not such an evil place. Sometimes it nearly weighs me down." She rested her forehead in her hand.

Unexpectedly he patted her arm in an unpracticed way that made it even more powerful. A knot formed in her throat.

"Verity, why do you care so much about Alec… about everyone?"

She looked into his solemn eyes and tilted her head. Was this the first time he'd called her by her given name? It felt so. Her stomach fluttered. "How can I not care that a young boy is suffering abuse at the hands of the father who should be loving and raising him to be a good man?"

"Orrin Dyke is not a good man."

The certainty in his tone did not lift her hopes. An unpleasant weight pressed on her lungs. *Poor Alec. Poor Mary.* "Thee doesn't think that Alec is spying for his father then?"

"I doubt it. He probably came just out of curiosity." Matthew withdrew his hand, but his touch lingered, startling Verity.

"I find it very odd that Virginians have no free schools. Didn't they see education as necessary for a knowledgeable electorate?"

He smiled in a way that twisted her heart. His smile mocked smiling. "The planters had the money and the power and they liked it that way."

"No doubt thee is right." She shook her head and rose, wishing she could help Matthew heal his wounds. *But it's not my place. Some pretty young maiden will do that.* "I will continue to pray about this. What we can do nothing about, our loving God will see to. Only He has the power to change hearts and minds. That is beyond us." *Thee is beyond me, Matthew. Whatever I have been feeling is not to be pursued. My heart is still with Roger. And thy heart is caught in the pain of the past.*

"Finally something we can agree on." Matthew had risen with her.

"I think, Matthew, that thee and I agree on many things." She said, smiling sadly. "I bid thee good night then, Matthew."

"Good night, ma'am."

She walked back to the house, burdened with the weight of all that had been unsaid.

"Fire! Fire!" The yells interrupted the Sunday-afternoon worship service at the Ransford plantation where Matt, Verity and her family were attending. Jolted, Matt spun around, trying to identify who was yelling. It sounded like the voice of a boy. Was it a prank?

The voice yelled again, "The Barnesworth barn is burning! Fire!"

That goaded Matt into action. He raced toward home. Behind him, he heard footsteps and shouting, but he didn't look back. He had over a mile to run.

Winded, he reached home first. Flames were devouring the stack of wood for the school and the frame they'd finished putting up yesterday, as well as the barn. For one second, he froze. Then he ran toward the pump halfway between the house and barn.

Verity and Samuel had arrived from the service. "We'll get buckets!" Verity called.

Matt began pumping. Samuel and Verity returned with fire buckets and wash buckets, handing them to those who'd followed.

Samuel took the place nearest the flaming barn and threw the first bucket of water on the fire, making it hiss. Verity, Beth and the others swarmed around the pump, letting the water from the pump fill their buckets. Then they formed a fire brigade line and began moving the buckets to Samuel and then back.

Soon a few of the nearest neighbors joined them. All was chaos—people shouting and coughing, the fire roaring like a giant beast. Their clothing and shoes became soaked with cold well water. Sparks and burning debris floated and swirled around their heads, stinging as they burned flesh. Matt pumped and pumped. His arms ached, threatening to cramp. Still, he pumped.

At last Joseph called, "I think it's out!"

Matt's arms hung at his sides, burning as if they'd caught fire. He emptied the bucket of water he'd been about to pass on over his sweaty head. His legs folded under him and he slid to the wet ground to sit. Panting, he looked around, exhausted.

It was a strange scene in the bright daylight. Over a dozen men, women, and children had helped fight the fire. They were either sitting on the ground as he was or they were leaning over with their hands propped against the tops of their knees. All were gasping. But farther in the distance, Matt was aware of people standing by, just watching.

This stunned him. Usually a whole town pitched in to help fight a fire. It could spread so easily that it endangered them all equally, no matter whose home it was. As he stared, a few of the figures moved away and disappeared. And as soon as they could stop gasping for breath, their nearest neighbors departed without a word of farewell or a backward glance.

Soon it was just Matt, Joseph, Verity, Elijah, Samuel, Hannah and the other former slaves who'd come to help. He gazed at the ruins of the barn and the charred remnants of the wood frame for the school. And then the stench hit him.

"I smell kerosene," Samuel said between gasps and coughs.

Matt nodded, rubbing his chest as if to loosen his constricted lungs. "It burned fast."

"What does thee mean?" Verity panted.

"I mean—" Matt turned his gaze on her "—someone poured kerosene on the barn, wood and school so the fire would destroy as much as possible before we got here."

Rage and sorrow warred in Matt's heart. It had started again.

Verity's face fell. Beth slumped against her mother on the ground, shivering and crying silently.

He stared at Verity. Her bonnet had slipped down to her shoulder. Her damp auburn curls had come undone, flowing over her slender shoulders. She looked paler than usual and her sodden clothing clung to her thin, wraithlike form. Just like his frail mother, all those years ago.

She shouldn't be here, facing this. It's too much for a woman. He'd have to protect her and her family. They were his responsibility. *I don't want to see her hurt.* He stopped there; going further would slice too close to the bone.

"Where are the horses?" Joseph asked, his face frighteningly red from the exertion. Matt had seen his father look like this before his death—it was a symptom of heart trouble. He worried that another event like this could be deadly for Joseph.

"The horses?" Matt looked around. Had their horses been stolen? Or had they perished in the fire?

"We'd have smelled the burning flesh if they'd been in the barn," Samuel said. "They should be safe."

"And we'd have heard them panic, too," Joseph added.

How about Beth's stray? Matt scanned the yard and saw the dog peering out from under the porch. Relief rolled through him like a tide.

"We thank all of thee for thy help," Verity said, looking around.

"Someone was bold enough to start this fire in broad daylight," Joseph said.

"And it probably wasn't just one person," Samuel added.

Elijah said with rich irony, "Do we need to discuss why someone wanted to burn down the barn, school and wood?"

Verity noted the sarcasm in Elijah's voice. "I knew they didn't want a school here," she said, "but don't they understand freedom of opinion?"

"No," Matt snapped. They hadn't fourteen years ago. Seeing dismay in her eyes sharpened his pain. This honest woman deserved better.

Samuel snorted. "General Robert E. Lee himself said that slavery had evil effects on both the slaves and their masters. You are quite right, ma'am. Some people here know nothing of freedom of any kind. Though slavery is gone, they cling to its vestiges in a blind passion."

"This is about reenslaving black people," Elijah stated. "They know that education will make that impossible."

"I do enjoy a good philosophical and political discussion," Joseph commented dryly, "but my back aches too much right now. We should be discussing what to do about our barn."

"We will have to build a new one," Verity said, rising and helping Beth up.

He'd known she'd say that. "We will. And we'll build the school, too." Matt turned to Elijah, determination flaming through him. "How many of your people would come to a barn raising this Saturday?" *No one's running me out of town again or hurting this woman and her family. Samuel said he's grown fangs, and it's about time I showed this town I have, too.*

Yesterday's fire still smoldering in his gut, Matt rode into town and hitched his horse. He strode into the general store that had been in Fiddlers Grove since 1776. Ironic, Matt thought. He wondered if anyone in town understood what had been won in the American Revolution. If they didn't, he was going to teach them today.

By setting his barn afire, someone had commenced the next battle for freedom. Matt was going to make it clear to Fiddlers Grove that he and Verity would win this battle. The Freedman's School would be built here.

The old men sitting outside on the store's bench rose, and followed Matt inside. The store was full of people and they instantly fell silent at Matt's entrance—again. Of course, the burning of his barn had been the topic of discussion this time. The town gathered at the general store. That's why Matt had chosen it as the place to announce his declaration of war.

He halted in the middle of the crowded store. And as one, they all drew back from him. He looked around, fixing his glare on each and every one in turn. "You all know about yesterday's fire. You probably know who set it. Now I have something else you all need to know. I'm going to telegraph the Yankee commander in Richmond today and ask for Union soldiers be sent to Fiddlers Grove *if* there is any more violent opposition to the Freedman's School. Your town will be occupied like Richmond." *You've messed with the wrong person. I'm not getting run out of town a second time.*

"You've got nerve telling us Negroes got to have a school," one old codger barked.

Another joined in, "Telling us that Negroes are going to vote. Hogs'll fly in Virginia first. You think you can tell us what to do—"

"I *can* tell you what will be done here. I've been authorized by the War Department to do just that." Matt felt the words fly from his mouth. Anger surged inside him as if it were a living thing.

"We're not going to ratify the amendments they're pushing through Congress. We got rights," the first codger objected, nearly dropping his pipe. "We're going to stand up for those rights in the Constitution."

"Did you care about my parents' rights when you forced them out of town?" Matt demanded, his frustration sparking inside him like a thunderbolt. "You lost the war and you're going to lose this battle, too. The South will change or suffer another war. Or worse. Mrs. Hardy and I are federal employees. Messing with us could send you to federal prison. Think about it."

Shocked silence was his only answer. He stalked out to his horse and mounted, galloping toward the next town and the telegraph office. In his mind, he saw Verity's frightened, smoke-smudged face. The image prompted him to dig his heels in and ride faster.

On the cloudy Second Day morning, the day after the horrible fire, Verity set out on her errand. She had meant to discuss what she planned to do today with Matthew, but he had ridden away just as she was about to start out. So she'd left on her business, praying for courage all the way. Yesterday's fire showed her that she must do something radical to reach out to the people of Fiddlers Grove. She had to take action, to stop the cycle of violence. She must turn the other cheek.

Now she walked resolutely up to the Ransford door and knocked, using the tarnished brass knocker twice. She glanced around, trying to calm her quivering stomach.

The door opened and an obviously shocked Elijah stared at her.

"Good day, Elijah. Are the Ransfords at home to guests?" Speaking these words sent another cascade of tremors through her. Did she have the nerve to do this?

Elijah's Adam's apple bobbed a few times as if he

were having trouble speaking. Finally he said, "I will inquire. Won't you step inside, ma'am?"

She smiled and stepped over the threshold. Elijah left her and she stared around the entry hall, noting that cobwebs hung from the candle lamp high above her. And dust collected in the corners of the room. Evidently the lady of this house did not dust.

"Why have you come here?"

Verity looked at Lirit Ransford, who was coming down the ornate curved staircase like a haughty princess in a fairy tale. "I bid thee good morning."

The pretty woman paused on the third step from the bottom. "I asked you why have you come here."

Verity refused to be daunted. After all, the worst that could happen was that Lirit Ransford would refuse the invitation.

When Matt arrived at the Barnesworth house, a sharp jab of hunger made him realize that he'd missed the noon meal. After unsaddling his horse, he bounded up the steps into the kitchen that had begun to feel like home, hoping Barney hadn't been given all the leftovers.

He found Verity sitting at the table, writing. He was immediately captivated by her small hand holding a pen. He recalled how tiny her hand had felt in his. Hannah stood by the stove, frowning. He stopped and waited for them to acknowledge him.

"I think Joseph will be able to bag us a wild turkey," Verity was saying. "And I brought pumpkins from Pennsylvania, so we'll have pumpkin pie." She looked up and welcomed Matt with a smile.

He'd never seen a smile more welcoming than Verity's. "Hello. I'm sorry I missed lunch," he began.

"Don't you worry yourself," Hannah said, reaching into the pie safe. "I kept something for you." She handed him a plate covered with a spotless kitchen cloth. "Wait till you hear the news."

He sat down, momentarily distracted by the sight of the plate heaped with ham, cornbread and jellied apple slices.

"I got dustin' to do if y'all excuse me." Hannah said, sounding disgruntled. She left them abruptly.

Matt looked to Verity. "Anything wrong?"

"Hannah doesn't approve of what I've done." Verity didn't give him any time to respond. "Where was thee off to this morning?"

Hunger and thirst came first. "Is that coffee?" He pointed to the pot on the stove.

"Yes." She made to rise.

"I'll get it." He went to the stove. "I'm used to waiting on myself."

"Thee is an unusual man, Matthew Ritter." She grinned.

Glad he'd made her smile for a change, Matt shrugged and sat down. "I sent a telegram to the commander in Richmond, telling him about the fire and alerting him that we might need troops if any more violent opposition occurs here."

Verity drew in breath, looking shocked. "Does thee think there will be more violent opposition?"

He paused to swallow the salty ham. "Yes, I think there's a good chance, especially since we're going to rebuild. I went to the general store before I left and warned everyone there what I was doing. The former slaves and their children are going to have a place to learn to read and write." His words bolstered his feeling of strength. "I didn't fight four long years—" *watch good men die* "—for my cousin to keep everything as it was before the war."

Verity looked worried. He chewed more slowly, trying to figure out what was going on. He recalled that Hannah had been upset with Verity. "Now, what did you do that Hannah doesn't like?" he asked, almost grinning. *How bad could it be?*

"This Thursday is Thanksgiving."

Thanksgiving? His family hadn't really celebrated this holiday. President Lincoln had it made a national observance in, what—'63? He nodded. "What about it?"

"Now that it's a national day devoted to giving thanks to God for the many blessings, I thought—"

Hannah walked into the room and asked in a huffy tone, "You tell him about that Thanksgiving dinner you planning?"

"Yes," Verity said, "I am."

"Did you tell Mr. Matt what you done this morning?" Hannah opened the oven and peered inside.

Hannah's words snatched away Matt's appetite. "What did you do?"

Verity looked him straight in the eye. "I invited thy cousin and his wife to share Thanksgiving dinner with us."

He felt his jaw drop. His fork clattered to the plate.

"And they accepted," Hannah pronounced, shaking her head with eyes heavenward.

Matt stared at Verity. Was the woman out of her mind?

Twilight was coming earlier now. Matthew had avoided Verity all day and had spoken to her in one-syllable words since her announcement. She walked toward his cabin, her soft shawl snug around her. They must discuss Thanksgiving. She must make him understand why she was doing this. But when she knocked on the closed cabin door, there was no answer. "Matthew, may I speak with thee?"

No reply.

She pulled her shawl even tighter around herself. The night would be a chilly one. She looked up and saw a trail of smoke coming out the chimney. "Matthew?" she tried once more.

No reply.

She stood there a few more moments and then walked back to the house. *I intended to discuss the invitation with thee, Matthew.*

Couldn't a family disagree on an issue yet remain friends? She'd married outside her parents' faith. Though they would have been happier if she'd wed another Friend, they had accepted Roger as a good man, as her choice of husband.

What had happened between the cousins? She sensed it must have something to do with the issue of slavery. Matthew's family had left when he was twelve. Samuel had run away at fifteen. What deep past wound had she opened up with this invitation?

The wind tugged her shawl, her hair. Pulling her shawl tighter, she bent her head into the wind and prayed for wisdom, blessing, love and healing to come to this town.

Chapter Eight

Thanksgiving morning

All morning Verity had helped Hannah in the kitchen with the Thanksgiving meal. She had just come up and changed into her best black dress before her guests arrived. Her guests, or her enemies?

Matthew had come in for breakfast before the rest of them and then vanished. Why, she wondered as she sat in front of the trifold mirror. She sighed at the wan reflection of her worried eyes. In the house that she'd grown up in, there had been no mirrors. As a child, the only time she had seen what her face looked like was when she glimpsed her reflection in the local creek on a sunny day.

This vanity had been her wedding gift from her husband. When she had objected that it was vanity indeed to look at oneself in a mirror, he had laughed and said that he wanted her to see how beautiful she was. And what a fortunate man he was.

She had been scandalized. It had taken a year before she could look into the mirror as she undid her hair every night and brushed it before braiding it again. She gazed at the daguerreotype of Roger on the vanity and pressed her fingers to his image. The sight of him gave her the confidence to face the situation she'd created. She knew a part of her would always love Roger, the father of her dear daughter. *But thee is gone, Roger. I will not see thee again till I see thee in eternity.*

She lifted the blue velvet box from one of the drawers. Opening it, she drew out and fastened the silver locket her husband had given her on their first anniversary. Maybe his giving her silver for the first anniversary had been an omen that they would never reach their silver anniversary. *No, I don't believe in omens. That's just foolish superstition.*

She needed armor today. The locket and the love it symbolized would protect her heart. *I must be bold like the apostle Paul. The Lord has not given me a spirit of fear.*

Fingering the cool oval locket, she heard the approach of a carriage. Would the Ransfords come in a carriage instead of walking? Recalling the haughty manner Lirit Ransford had displayed three days ago when Verity had invited her, she wouldn't be surprised.

The rag-doll feeling came over her again. It was as if she were being moved by outside forces. Was this because being a confronter was not what she wanted to be? Sighing, Verity rose and walked to the top of the stairs. The scents of sage, nutmeg and cinnamon hung tantalizingly in the air. Verity wished her appetite would come back and banish the panic roiling in her stomach. Beth stood next to her on tiptoe, looking over the railing on the landing. Verity offered Beth her hand. "Let's go welcome our guests."

Her daughter gave her a quizzical look. Verity took Beth's small hand and led her down. The girl had picked up on the undercurrent of tension that had run steadily in this house the past two days. As they walked hand in hand down the stairs, Verity wondered if Matthew would come or stay in his cabin. She and Beth stepped down into the entrance hall just as Hannah opened the door. An icy wave of apprehension washed through Verity.

She put on her brightest smile. "Good day! Welcome to our home."

Hannah said nothing as she stalked away toward the kitchen. Her stiff back announced to all her attitude toward this "nonsense." Beth hid behind Verity's skirt. Verity stroked her fine dark hair, trying to reassure her. "Dacian and Lirit, I'm so happy thee have come to share our Thanksgiving meal."

Dacian closed the door against the stiff breeze, took

off his hat and hung it on the hall tree. "Good day, Mrs. Hardy." He bowed. "And I'm happy to meet your pretty little daughter."

"Yes, Beth, this is Dacian Ransford and his wife, Lirit." Verity offered him her trembling hand. Beth curtsied.

"I don't know why you think you may address me by my given name," Lirit Ransford snapped.

"I beg thy pardon," Verity said, controlling the quaver just beneath her words. "I was raised a Friend and we never use titles. Of course, if thee prefers, I will call thee Mrs. Ransford. I don't wish to cause—"

"You may do that, then," Lirit cut in. "And I shall call you—" the woman paused, giving her a taunting look "—Mrs. Foolhardy."

"Lirit," Dacian cautioned her in a low voice.

Mrs. Ransford lifted her chin, unrepentant.

Oddly the unmasking of the woman's hostility steadied Verity. "Thee may call me Verity or Mrs. Hardy or whatever thee thinks best, Mrs. Ransford," Verity said with dignity. "Won't thee please come into the parlor?"

"Ladies," Dacian said, and motioned for them to precede him. Soon they were all seated in the parlor— the Ransfords on the sagging sofa and Verity with Beth on the worn love seat across from them. The Barnesworth parlor was a mix of tattered upholstered furniture, Chippendale and primitive pieces obviously crafted by a local woodworker. A stiff silence settled over them. Beth didn't even fidget.

Help me, Lord. Verity cleared her throat. "Today may be a holiday new to thee."

"Yes, it is, ma'am," Dacian said.

"We've never celebrated Yankee holidays," Mrs. Ransford said, her low opinion of such things evident in her arrogant tone. She sneered when she looked around at the dilapidated parlor. The wallpaper was faded and peeling in places.

Verity had itched to do some upkeep on it, but she was here to teach and begin God's work of healing, not to strip wallpaper and paint walls. *Please, Matthew, come help me. Thee knows these people. I don't.* Verity tried again, saying, "We are one nation again and so Virginians can celebrate Thanksgiving also."

Mrs. Ransford sniffed.

"I believe that we can all agree that having the war ended at last is something to celebrate," Verity ventured, her misgivings over issuing this invitation expanding moment by moment.

"Yes, ma'am. I take it that you are a widow," Dacian said, obviously trying to make conversation.

Her throat convulsed, but she forced out, "Yes, my husband fell at the Second Battle of Bull Run."

"I believe we called that the Second Battle at Manassas," Dacian said.

Mrs. Ransford's face flushed. "I lost my only

brother in that battle." She glared at Verity. "Maybe your husband killed Geoffrey."

The woman's bald words snapped Verity's composure, her hand itching to slap Lirit's sneering face.

"Who can tell who shot whom in the midst of a battle," Dacian said solemnly. "I try not to think of all the men I killed."

His grave words sluiced over Verity like a bucket of icy water. Pain spiraled through her, bringing tears. The four years of the war had been the worst of her life. She pulled out her handkerchief and dabbed at her eyes. "The war was horrible. That's why I invited thee here today. The war must end. Healing must begin."

"Yes," the man agreed.

Beth looked back and forth between the two women. "Who did my papa kill? Who's Geoffrey?"

Not looking at Lirit, Verity wiped her eyes and patted Beth's hand. "Thee must not take all we say at face value. No one knows how or why Mrs. Ransford's brother fell in battle but God."

Mrs. Ransford had conscience enough to look abashed. "I didn't mean anything bad about your father, little girl."

Verity took advantage of the shift in this proud woman's tone. "I've been wanting to get to know the women of this town. Are there any ladies' sewing groups or mission societies here?"

Mrs. Ransford's face lifted in an unhappy mix of

smugness and derision. "I'm hosting the next meeting of the Daughters of the Confederacy Monday next at three in the afternoon. I'm sure you would be welcomed with open arms." Thick sarcasm oozed from every word, her face smug and condescending.

Verity swallowed a hasty retort, holding on to her patience. She knew this wouldn't be easy. But love always triumphed over evil if one held on. Christ had won the victory over sin and death by holding on in the face of cruel mocking, torture and the cross.

The memory of the fire just days ago had finally convinced Verity that some in Fiddlers Grove would not hesitate to hurt her if they could get away with it. Still, she must do what she thought God had called her to do. It was possible that Lirit Ransford could help her with her personal mission—the meeting she was hosting could prove the perfect opportunity, as strange as that might seem. "Thank you, Mrs. Ransford, for the kind invitation."

The woman opened her mouth, but Matthew appeared in the entrance to the parlor, sparing Verity from further insult. Both Ransfords stared at him. He was dressed in his Sunday clothes and looked very handsome. Joy and uncertainty clashed within Verity as she rose to greet him.

"Matthew, I'm so glad thee has come."

"I wouldn't miss dinner." Matthew strode into the room and halted in front of his cousin. "I see you came to celebrate Thanksgiving with us." Matthew's wry tone nearly matched Mrs. Ransford's mocking words.

Oh, dear. What have I done? Verity realized her fingernails were digging into her own flesh.

Dacian met Matthew's gaze but gave no indication of sentiment for or against his cousin.

Hannah stomped down the hall to the parlor entrance. "Dinner's ready."

Verity wished Hannah wouldn't make her negative opinion quite so evident. Completely devoid of appetite, she rose. "Won't thee please come to the dining room?"

Joseph appeared in the hall, carrying the platter with the golden-brown roast turkey. "Hello, hello," he greeted the guests, nodding them into the dining room across the hall. Joseph set the platter in the middle of the table, laid with the Barnesworth chipped china and a centerpiece of fall leaves and acorns that Beth had gathered. Then Joseph shook hands with Dacian and bowed to his wife.

Soon Joseph had everyone seated and he offered grace. Verity could only be grateful for Joseph's imperturbable cheerfulness. The delicious aromas seemed to affect everyone. Mrs. Ransford almost smiled while Joseph carved. The dishes passed from hand to hand while Joseph entertained them with the story of the merry chase the flock of wild turkeys had led him on.

As she listened to the story, Verity kept one eye on Matthew. He said not a word but twice looked at his pocket watch. Why? She took her first mouthful of creamy mashed potatoes. And then a knock came at the door.

Matthew rose. "I'll get it, Hannah!" he called, and went to the door.

Verity froze, her fork in midair, as she recognized the voice of the person Matthew had just ushered inside. *Oh, no.*

Then Matthew returned. "Since you invited guests to join us for Thanksgiving dinner, Mrs. Hardy, I felt free to do so, as well." He stepped aside and there was Samuel, standing in her dining room.

The reaction was instant. Mrs. Ransford leaped to her feet. "I won't tolerate an insult like this. I'm leaving." She threw down her linen napkin. "Dacian, take me home."

Dacian remained motionless. A raw, dangerous silence hovered over the holiday table. Verity's heart pounded. Then Dacian said to Verity, "Ma'am, did you do this to insult us?"

Verity didn't like his equating sitting with Samuel, a good man, with an insult. Maybe she had been foolish. What good could one meal do in face of such prejudice? She looked Dacian Ransford directly in the eye. "I invited thee because after our barn was burned, I felt I had to do something positive to end the violence. I was hoping that somehow at this meal I could start to reach out to this community, to soften not harden hearts. We've already discussed frankly why I came here, Dacian."

The ugly silence in the room continued. Then Matthew broke it and said, sounding disgusted, "She's an idealist, Dace. She can't help herself—"

His voice was drowned out by Barney's frantic barking just outside the dining-room window. Verity stiffened. What now?

Beth leaped up. "That's Barney! Maybe those bad men who burned our barn came back!" The little girl raced from the room. "They might hurt Barney!"

"Beth! Wait!" Shock and caution pulsing through her veins, Verity jumped up, racing after her daughter. "Beth!"

Outside the back door, Verity paused. Ahead still barking wildly, Barney was now running with Beth toward the cabin. Verity chased after Beth, aware that Matthew was right behind her, followed by Samuel and Dacian.

The cabin door was open. Verity burst inside to see Barney panting and whining near the bed. Beth stood beside him. "Mama, somebody hurt that boy Alec." Beth's voice was high and thin. "Mama, he's bleeding."

Verity's hands flew to her mouth, stifling a gasp. Alec lay halfway on Matthew's narrow bed. Blood dripped from his mouth onto the floor and both his eyes were swollen nearly shut.

"Mama, is the boy going to die?" Beth's voice was shrill. "Mama?"

Verity went to her and pulled her close, her pulse leaping and stuttering. *Dear Father, this poor boy.* "No, we will make him better." She turned to Matthew standing in the doorway. "Please, will you carry him to the house?" She could not hide the strain in her voice. She sounded as if she were tightening a stubborn screw. She felt like it. *Oh, Lord, this cruelty is so hard to witness. What can I do to stop this suffering?*

Verity pressed Beth's back against her to make room for Matthew. He scooped the boy into his arms and headed for the main house. Within minutes, Verity was breathing hard and fighting back tears as she followed Matthew up the stairs. She looked back at Samuel, Dacian, Joseph and Beth standing in the hall at the foot of the stairs. She held back tears and tried to look calm. "Please go back in and eat. Beth, stay with your grandfather and entertain our guests." She didn't wait for a response.

Matt took Alec directly to Beth's room. He waited for Verity to turn down the bedding, then he gently laid the boy on the canopied bed, wishing he could do more. He stood back as she examined the boy yet again, touching her hand to his forehead, pressing her ear against his thin chest to listen to his heart, and then moving his limbs. When she tried to move Alec's right arm, he moaned. She very carefully moved her fingers around the elbow joint and then probed up and down the length of the arm. "He may have a break in his arm."

Matt felt sickened at the sight of the boy's battered face.

Hannah hustled into the room with a wash basin, rolled bandages and some small brown corked bottles of medicine. Samuel followed her with a kettle of hot water, steam still puffing from its spout. "How is that boy?" Hannah's voice was soft, muted.

Verity turned. "Thank thee, Hannah and Samuel. That's just what I need. I can handle this with Matthew's assistance. Please go down and make sure our guests have everything they need. And please watch over Beth. Seeing this has upset her. She has bad memories—we nursed soldiers after Gettysburg. She has a soft heart."

"Just like her mother," Samuel said, and Matt silently echoed the sentiment. Matt's chest tightened into a painful knot. He tried to imagine what a very little girl would recall of the noise of battle and bloodied wounded. The thought of Beth having to witness the horror of war was almost more than he could bear.

Verity smiled. "Thank thee both."

Samuel and his mother left them. Matt hovered near Verity, ready to do whatever she needed. He watched her bathe the boy's face and dab tincture of iodine on the many cuts. Alec seemed to be awake but unresponsive. He winced at the iodine but made no outcry. Matt's thoughts turned to Mary. Was she safe or lying somewhere bruised and bleeding, too?

"Matthew, would thee undress Alec while I go get a nightshirt from Joseph's room?"

"I got…to go home," Alec finally whispered, wincing with pain at each word. "I just…came to get away. And you helped…me last time."

Matt moved closer to the bed. Anger was replacing shock and gathering tight and hot in his gut.

"Thee will go home when thee is better," Verity said in a no-nonsense tone.

"My ma," the boy moaned. "She needs me."

Verity gave Matt a significant look and left the room.

Matt reached to unbutton Alec's threadbare, blood-spattered shirt. No one should have let sweet Mary McKay wed Orrin Dyke.

"Sir, please—"

Matt made his voice strong and sure. "Mr. Ransford is downstairs, Alec. He will make sure your ma is protected. Now lie still and don't argue. You did right coming here."

The boy passed out. Matt quickly undressed him and pulled the blanket over his bruised body. Verity entered with the nightshirt. "Will thee help me put it on him?"

Matt supported the boy's neck and shoulders while Verity pulled the nightshirt over his head and arms. Her motions were efficient yet gentle and motherly. Watching her tend to Alec attracted him in a new, more powerful way. She might be an idealist, but when faced with dreadful reality, she knew how to handle it.

As he watched her hands move, he could almost feel her gentle touch soothing him also. After the nightshirt was on, she took a linen towel and fashioned a sling, which she tied around the boy's right arm. Then she stepped back and looked up at Matt. "Something must be done for this child."

He nodded, unable to speak because of the anger surging up like hot air from a bellows.

There was a knock at the door and Samuel stepped inside. "I'm going to sit with the boy while you two go down and eat." He held up a hand. "My mother's orders. Don't think you can go against her. She wants you downstairs and me upstairs."

Matt hesitated. He'd done right by inviting Samuel—and he'd done wrong. His reactions tangled inside him like a kite's string caught in the branches of a tree.

Verity nodded and walked to the door. As she passed Samuel, she patted his arm. Matt followed her down to the dining room. She paused at the doorway. Looking over her shoulder, Matt glimpsed Joseph at the head of the table with the Ransfords to his right and Beth to his left. They were eating pumpkin pie and whipped cream. Matt's mouth watered at the scent of nutmeg and cinnamon, but his stomach clenched at facing Dace and Lirit again.

"How is Alec, Mama?" Beth asked, her face drawn and worried.

Matt seated Verity at her place and then sat by her side, across from his cousin. Hannah bustled in and put down plates of food in front of Verity and him. "I put your plates in the oven so they kept warm."

"Thank you, Hannah," Verity said with a sigh.

Matt didn't like how tired and worn down she sounded. But what could he do about that? What could he do for Alec? He picked up his fork and began eating, hardly tasting his food.

"How's the boy, Mama?" Beth asked again.

Matt chewed slowly, waiting for Verity to answer.

"He's resting," Verity replied, her fork motionless in her hand. "Has thee finished eating?"

"Yes. Thank you. May I please be excused to go see Alec?" Beth asked, sitting on the edge of her chair.

"I think thee had better go out and play with Barney. He is moping around the back porch for thee. And after all, he must be rewarded for letting us know Alec needed our help."

"You want me to go and play with Barney?" Beth asked, rising.

Verity nodded. Beth curtsied to the Ransfords and left the room.

Matt touched Verity's arm. "Eat. Don't let your

food go cold. Hannah will have a fit." Verity nodded, her lower lip trembling.

"Will someone please tell me what is going on in this crazy house?" Lirit demanded.

Matt waited for Verity to reply, but she merely began eating. He found he could contain himself no longer. "Orrin Dyke is abusing his son. We found Alec beaten in my cabin back by the barn. We brought him inside and Verity—Mrs. Hardy has treated his wounds."

"Well, what can you expect from trash like Orrin Dyke," Lirit said dismissively.

"Calling names doesn't help the boy," Dace said.

"The boy isn't our responsibility," Lirit snapped back.

Verity looked up and fixed Lirit with an unwavering stare. Lirit blushed finally and looked down at her plate. "Dace, I think it's time you took me home. It appears that Mrs. Hardy has other matters to attend to," she said.

Dace gazed at his wife. "Very well. I'll take you home, Lirit, but then I will return here."

"Why?" Lirit pouted.

"Because I am still Dacian Ransford, and the welfare of Mary Dyke's son is my concern. The Ransfords have always taken care of the people in this county. And may I remind you, you are a Ransford, too."

The Ransfords had always taken care of the *white* people in this county, Matt silently amended.

Lirit rose in a huff. Matt had never liked Lirit much, and he liked her even less now. He recalled all the times when they were children and she'd ruined their fun with tears and tattling. Some people never changed.

Joseph said with gallantry, "If you will trust me with your lovely wife and team, Mr. Ransford, I'll drive your lady home and then return with the carriage."

"Thank you," Dace said. "Lirit, I will be home as soon as matters here are concluded." Face averted, Lirit swept from the room without thanking Verity for the meal. Joseph hurried to help her into her cape in the hall. Dace stared down at the remains of his pumpkin pie and cup of coffee.

Matt pitied his cousin, married to such a woman. Why had Dace married Lirit anyway? *When I marry, I...* He found he could not finish the thought, it startled him so.

When Joseph and Lirit had gone, Dace looked up. "What do you think we should do about this, Matt? I can confront Orrin, but—" Dace paused and then continued, sounding bitter. "I don't have the clout I once had in this town. Money is power and I don't have the money I once had."

Caught up short, Matt could hardly believe his cousin had just admitted this.

"I think that thee still has thy position in the community. Thee still owns thy land," Verity said.

"She's right." Matt added. "You're still the Ransford. Your father's family has been the most prominent in this county for over a hundred years." The memory of Dace's father fanned the flame smoldering inside Matt. Why hadn't he weighed in on the side of Matt's family? Then Matt chided himself. *What has that got to do with the present, with Alec and Mary? This is about their horrible situation, not ancient history.*

Dace looked from Matt to Verity. "I'll go talk to Orrin. But what if it just spurs him to more cruelty? What if he turns violence onto Mary, too?"

"What makes you think he hasn't already?" Matt asked, thinking of how Alec was always concerned about his mother.

"Yes, I'm afraid that a man who beats his son usually mistreats his wife, too," Verity said. "I'm pleased that both of you want to do something for Alec and Mary. My family has tried to help women in this type of home situation in the past. And unfortunately they have been actively opposed and criticized for interfering with a husband's right to rule his home."

Dace lifted his chin. "A man who strikes a woman or beats a child in this manner is a cad, and every right-thinking man should agree."

So his cousin had learned some compassion over the years. Matt finished his meal and then accepted pumpkin pie from a sober-looking Hannah. Dace stirred his coffee and stared into it moodily. Verity spoke of her family in Pennsylvania, evidently trying to salvage the ruined holiday. Her soft voice soothed him. When she finished eating and excused herself to go up and check on the boy, Dace and Matt sat across from each other alone in the quiet room.

Dace broke the silence. "You invited Samuel to insult me, didn't you?"

"Interestingly, my main intention was to demonstrate to Mrs. Hardy how impossible it is to do what she wants to do here. She wants to bring peace and reconciliation, and make people accept the changes that are coming. Mrs. Hardy is an idealist, not a realist."

"She told me that, too." Dace stirred his coffee, watching the spoon swirl the dark brew.

"And we both know it's impossible, don't we?" Matt pressed his cousin.

Dace didn't respond, but his expression said Matt was right. The sound of the returning carriage gave Dace a reason to leave. "I'll go have a word with Dyke. Please thank Mrs. Hardy for the best meal I've eaten in a very long time. And my compliments to your cook."

Matt rose and nodded.

After Dace had left, Matt stood in the hallway, listening to the quiet. Then he mounted the steps one by one, drawn against his will to the gracious woman of the house.

Chapter Nine

Matt found Verity alone—Samuel must have gone down to the kitchen. Matt stood for a moment in the open doorway, wanting to say something comforting but not knowing what. Then he noticed her shoulders were shaking. It rent his heart in twain.

With two long strides, he was at her side and she was in his arms. "Don't cry. Don't cry," he murmured, breathing in her familiar lavender fragrance.

The top of her head just brushed his chin. The sensation of her springy hair against that sensitive area made it hard for him to draw breath. He stroked her hair and felt its fullness and life. She was so small, so slight that he felt he must be careful not to hold her too close, to crush her. How could a woman so small have such big ideas, such passion to help others? How did she bear all that compassion and all the pain caring brought?

Her weeping slowed, and then she was looking up at him. The tears glistening in her eyes only added to her beauty. He could see each tear in her lashes and her eyes were the perfect shade of brown, so warm and confiding. He pressed her closer, gently, as if holding a living bird in his hands. Her forehead was right next to his lips now. If he moved only a fraction of an inch, they would touch her, kiss her.

Sanity hit him. He released her slowly, reluctantly. If he gave in to temptation and kissed her, their whole relationship would change. *We have to work together. And I won't lead her to believe there might be something more for us.*

She stepped back and looked down, wiping her eyes with a handkerchief. "I'm sorry for breaking down like that. It's just hard to see a child suffer so."

Matt tried to speak, but his throat was too thick. He cleared it and tried again. "Dace has gone to confront Dyke."

She looked up at him quickly, her face full of worry. "I must pray about that." And right before his eyes, she dropped to her knees, put her hand on Alec's shoulder and bowed her head.

He watched her, hoping God was hearing her and would not let more harm come to Alec and Mary. He bowed his head, too. *God, this woman has enough to worry about without this. Let Dace succeed in putting the fear of You in Orrin.* He looked up. It had been a long time since he'd prayed.

Verity rose and turned to him. "I'm sorry I didn't discuss inviting thy cousin and his wife to dinner today. On First Day, I truly intended to, but thee went off and I didn't want to wait to issue the invitation. I felt the Spirit moving me to go to them."

"And I'm sorry I invited Samuel only to upset Dace and Lirit." And honesty forced him to add, "And you."

She rested one of her delicate hands on his arm. "Thee is a good man, Matthew Ritter. But thee spent four years learning to kill, suffering overwhelming horror and grief day by day. Does thee think I know nothing of war? Our farm was only a short distance from the battleground of Gettysburg. Beautiful green farmland turned into a killing field." A tremor visibly shuddered through her. "I can think of nothing worse than war." She gripped his arm. "I want to bind up our nation's wounds as President Lincoln bade us. And I think, Matthew, that thee came to Fiddlers Grove to do the same."

"There can be no binding up here," Matt said, his voice hoarse. He hated showing evidence of emotion. But her hand was warm upon his flesh and he seemed to lose himself in the sensation.

She squeezed his arm and then turned back to Alec. "We shall see, Matthew Ritter. We shall see."

* * *

Matt sat at his table and wrote in his journal, a habit his parents had started him on when he learned to write. He found that writing down his thoughts often helped him see what he should do next, and he was hoping for some clarity about the boy. The journal didn't help this time, unfortunately. He heard the sound of the carriage and walked to the door to see Dace. Dace didn't get down, so Matt went to meet him. The wind chilled him in his shirtsleeves.

"I talked to Dyke."

Matt read grimness in his cousin's face. It chilled him more than the wind. "How did he take it?"

"Not good. He told me Alec was his business. And reminded me I wasn't his boss." Dace slapped the reins and began to turn his carriage toward home. "He'll want revenge on someone. Watch your back."

On the sunny but chilly Seventh Day morning, Verity stood on her back porch and gazed at a stack of new lumber, which stood beside the charred, acrid-smelling remains of the burned barn. Her outward calm was thinner than eggshell.

The wood had been delivered yesterday. Today, many men had come with shovels, saws and hammers. Along with Matthew and Samuel, they milled around her yard, laughing and joking amidst the ruins. Today, they would raise the new barn. In the coming week, the school would rise. And just in time since the chill of the west wind would soon make school on the porch impossible.

Verity couldn't help but notice that Matthew's was the only white face in the yard. She looked up the road once more. If only one white man from the town came to help today, she wouldn't have this deep worry gnawing at her. She still hoped that Dacian would make an appearance today.

"Good day, Elijah, Hannah," she greeted the couple as she walked down the few steps. She tried to smile, but it was a poor, wobbly attempt. She'd spent most of the night praying for God's protection for Matthew, her family and the people who'd come out today to rebuild their barn. But she'd experienced that awful feeling that her prayers had hit the ceiling and fallen back onto her head.

"Good morning, ma'am," Elijah replied. "I've come though I've never built anything in my life. I hope I'll be a help rather than a hindrance."

Hannah must have sensed Verity's low spirits, because she came alongside her and gave her a hearty hug. "You be all right. Everything be all right. God is here today."

Verity smiled, but could not shake the image of the barn burning. The memory left her sapped and shaken as if she were just recovering from a fever.

Though Matthew had said little, Verity knew Orrin

Dyke would strike back at them. Alec was still asking to go home, but Verity had insisted he stay. And with a badly sprained ankle and a broken arm, he couldn't get home by himself.

She'd not overheard Matthew and his cousin, but she'd seen the two of them talking late on Thanksgiving evening from the window. Dacian Ransford had gone to confront Orrin Dyke, and he had not looked encouraged as he'd driven away.

Lord, please, if there's more trouble, Matthew will telegraph for troops and Fiddlers Grove will become a battlefield. The animosity will grow and fester. Please foil any attempts to stop us from building the barn and then the school. No feeling of peace came.

Elijah, Hannah and Verity obeyed Joseph's beckoning wave and joined the circle of men and women around the burned remnants. "Brother Elijah, would you offer a prayer for our work today?" Joseph asked, doffing his hat. Matthew stood beside Verity, looking dour.

Verity noticed his rifle propped against a nearby tree and a pistol on his belt. The sight of the guns upset her, but when she looked at Matthew, she was overcome by the memory of him at Alec's bedside on Thanksgiving afternoon. She hoped no one noticed her warm blush as she remembered the feel of Matthew's arms around her.

Elijah prayed for strength and safety. At the end,

everyone said, "Amen." Then she and Hannah went inside. Joseph had bought her another dozen chickens. It would take all morning to dress, fry and get them on the table, along with cornbread, turnips and apple pies to feed the workers.

On her way inside, she glimpsed movement beyond the trees around her property. A few white men were just standing there, watching. Were they gathering for an attack? Or was this just intimidation? She recalled the terrible scene the day before she'd left Pennsylvania when Roger's cousin had spewed such hateful words about what they'd do to her here in Dixie. She met Hannah's troubled eyes, which probably bore a resemblance to her own.

"Think they'll do anything today?" Hannah muttered.

Verity shrugged, unable to say a word, her throat tight. Who knew? Just in case, someone came to cause trouble, she'd ordered Beth to stay inside with Barney and keep Alec company upstairs. The boy was still in too much pain to go home, and Verity worried Orrin Dyke would lash out at the boy because of Dacian's interference.

"Well, Hannah, we have food to prepare," Verity said, and turned toward the kitchen. A few of Hannah's friends were waiting there, having come to help with the cooking while their husbands worked on the barn.

The sounds of saws and hammers continued all morning. Verity filled the pie crusts with apples and sugar, chatting with the women as they fried the chickens and peeled the turnips. But through the windows, she kept track of the white men gathering in the shelter of the trees around her property.

Their number had been steadily increasing all morning. And now a few had begun taunting the men working outside. Verity's stomach knotted. She could practically see the flames and smell the kerosene. *But what choice do we have, Lord, but to rebuild? The horses must have shelter in the winter. And we must build the school. We can't give in and run away.*

To distract herself, Verity asked, "Have any of thee women ever heard about the movement for women's suffrage?"

More taunts outside. Verity tasted blood and realized that she'd bitten her lower lip.

"What suffrage?" one of the women asked. "Don't sound good."

"Suffrage means the right to vote," Verity answered. "Women deserve the right to vote just as much as men. We're just as smart as they are."

"Smarter," Hannah said with a grin. "We have to be." All the women chuckled.

The volume of the taunts suddenly escalated and Verity could hear threats, racial epithets and foul words. The women in the kitchen fell silent. Then

Verity realized that she wasn't the only one who was worried. Each face around her looked strained. The chatter had been their attempt to deny what was happening. And what might happen.

"What we going to do if someone try to stop our menfolk?" Hannah put the overwhelming question into words.

Verity gave up the pretense of working on the pies, wiping her hands on a dish cloth. Alarm coursed through her. She braced herself, drawing up her strength. "Nothing is going to happen. Matthew made it quite clear that he'd telegraph for Union troops if—"

A rock crashed through the kitchen window. The women screamed as one. *Dear Father,* Verity prayed silently. A rifle shot sounded. And then another. Beth screamed upstairs. And Barney was barking wildly again. Heart pounding, Verity ran into the hall and up the stairs to her daughter.

Matt had expected trouble. Counting the white men gathering around them had been like watching storm clouds roll in. And now the thunder and lightning had started. Firing his pistol at the first man to shoot, Matt ran for cover and grabbed his rifle. He hefted it to his shoulder. A shot thudded into the tree above his head. Had he survived four years of war just to die here? The familiar crosscurrents of wanting to fly to cover and forcing himself to face enemy fire twisted inside him.

Matt aimed and fired. All around him a free-for-all had broken out. White men were struggling with black men, who were fighting back with bare fists, hammers and shovels. He aimed for the few snipers who sheltered behind the big oaks and were trying to pick off as many black men as they could. He glimpsed the red of a shirt near one trunk, fired and heard a yell. He kept firing toward the trees that concealed the snipers. Finally, the shooting stopped. He reloaded his rifle, watching for more sniper fire.

He was glad Verity, Beth, Hannah and the rest of the women were safe in the house. Then, out of the corner of his eye, Matt glimpsed Orrin running toward the front of the house.

No, you don't. Matt raced after him, stopping twice to shoot as sniper fire started again. Finally he bounded inside the widow's front door and saw Orrin crouched on the floor, starting a fire on the parlor rug.

Matt lifted his rifle. "Stop. Smother that. And step away, Dyke."

The bigger man roared and charged at Matt. Matt hit Orrin's jaw with his rifle butt. Orrin jerked, but it didn't stop him. He slammed Matt back against the wall, his hands around Matt's neck.

Matt gasped for air, jamming his rifle butt into

Orrin's belly and shoving forward. *I have to put out the fire.*

Orrin wrenched Matt's rifle from him. Matt landed another blow on Orrin's jaw and knocked the rifle out of Orrin's hand. Then it was fist to fist. Matt kept punching. Orrin pounded him, his fists like flat irons—it was like fighting a bear.

Verity ran down the steps. "Stop!" she shouted. "Fire!"

Neither man paid any attention to her. Matt kept maneuvering for more room. Finally, he was able to grab his rifle off the floor. "Put your hands over your head or I shoot!" The fire had now engulfed the rug.

Orrin shouted and lunged toward Verity. Matt shot but missed. Orrin grabbed Verity and held her in front of him. "Get back! Or I'll snap her neck!"

Matt blazed with anger. The sofa near him was catching fire. "Get your filthy hands off her!"

"No! You drop your rifle! Or I snap her neck!" Orrin pressed Verity back against him with one arm around her neck.

Samuel burst through the door.

Orrin bellowed with rage, threw Verity at Matt and lunged for Samuel.

By the time Matt got to his feet and helped Verity up, Orrin had run outside. Samuel was unconscious in the entry hall. Smoke billowed up from the hungry flames devouring the carpet. Grabbing up the rag rug in front of the open door, Matt began beating out the rug and sofa fire.

Verity knelt beside Samuel's body. "Wake up!" she shouted, shaking him. "Fire!" Then, hearing Barney barking, she called up the stairs. "Beth! Alec! The house is afire! Run outside!"

Finally Samuel blinked, moaned and sat up.

Verity left him, got a small rug from the dining room and ran to Matt. Side by side, they beat out the sofa fire. Coughing, choking, Matt tried to speak to Verity but couldn't. She leaned over, rubbing her neck where Orrin had held her tightly. Samuel helped Matthew drag the smoking sofa outside. Verity joined them in the welcome fresh air.

Verity looked toward Matt and gasped—one of his eyes was swollen shut and his lips were split and bleeding. But he was breathing and standing. She looked beyond the porch and was crushed by what she saw. Many had fallen in the gun battle. Fear pierced her like an ice pick. Beyond the porch, Hannah was kneeling beside Elijah on the ground. "Did any die?" Verity called to her.

Hannah stood. "I don't think so, but we got a few shot and the rest are beaten up pretty bad." Samuel started toward his mother.

Matthew went back in the house and then tossed what was left of the parlor rug into the yard. "Samuel," he called, "go and see who needs help most. Then bring them inside. We'll use the dining room and parlor as a field hospital. The fire burned the rug and scorched the sofa, but it didn't get to the walls. We can be glad that Orrin doesn't know much about setting fires without kerosene."

Verity hurried to help Samuel. As she examined each man lying or slumped on the grass around their yard, visions of Gettysburg flashed in her mind. All this over a barn raising. Those who were able to walk headed home on foot in groups. Verity could see white men carrying their wounded away through the trees. Matt and Samuel were bringing the injured inside where Hannah quickly began treating wounds. Verity hoped her nursing supplies would hold out.

After Joseph, Beth, with Barney beside her, and Alec had been in bed for many hours, Matt, Verity and Samuel sat around the kitchen table, too exhausted to move. Hannah was sleeping in the parlor on a rocking chair and footstool, keeping watch over the few men who didn't have family to nurse them. With a bandaged head, Elijah had gone back to their cabin without her.

Matt tried not to stare at Verity. Everything in him wanted desperately to hold her tight. His determination to protect her had only grown more fierce as the danger increased. "In the morning, I'm going to telegraph the commander in Richmond that we need troops here so we can build the barn and school," Matthew said harshly.

"Be sure you're armed," Samuel warned. "Orrin might try to ambush you if you give him half a chance."

"Don't worry. I'll be ready for anything." Matt was assaulted by the image of Orrin Dyke holding Verity, ready to kill her. He gripped the cup so tightly that his knuckles turned white.

A soft hand touched his. "Is thee all right? I can put a cold compress on thy eye again."

His gaze connected with Verity's and the tender concern in her eyes nearly unmanned him; tears he wouldn't shed collected behind his eyes. "I'll be all right," he said, sounding gruff and unfriendly to his own ears.

She squeezed his hand and then let go. "It seems people here haven't had enough of violence."

"Evidently not," Samuel said, lifting his coffee to his bettered mouth. His arms were so tired, his hands shook.

Matt was so glad Samuel had been at the barn raising. He was still a friend and had stood by them. *I should probably be glad that Dace stayed away. At least he didn't join in the attack.*

Verity leaned her head into her hand. "We should go to bed." But neither she nor Samuel nor Matt moved.

In the lamplight, Matt gazed at Verity. Her copper hair had come down completely and the long waves made a curtain that hid her face. *Orrin Dyke, you will never touch another hair on her head.*

Samuel rotated his neck as if it hurt. "I'll stay here tomorrow, Matt, while you head to the telegraph office. And you should ask for an army doctor. A couple of the wounded need professional care."

Matt nodded.

"Where will this all end?" Verity whispered, her brown eyes lifted to him.

Matt had no answer for her. He knew Fiddlers Grove would lose this battle in the end, but at what cost to the town and to the three of them around the table?

"I don't know the final outcome, but I do know you are doing what is right," Samuel said. "Good people cannot give in to evil. Where would I be if Matt's family hadn't spoke out against slavery and its injustice, or if your family hadn't joined the Underground Railroad? Hadn't helped me to freedom? Hadn't been willing to fight a war?"

Matt nodded, gripping his cup so he wouldn't reach for Verity's hand. They were colleagues and should remain so. "We can't give up."

Verity nodded. "I'm going to see if I can get a few hours of rest." She staggered to her feet.

Matt rose and grasped her arm to steady her. "I'll help you."

"No," she said, touching his arm, "I can make it. I want to check on our patients first anyway."

Matt knew that if they had been alone, he would have pulled her close and held her. *Not a good idea.* She left the room, her light footsteps quiet in the hallway.

Samuel rose, too. "I'm going to sleep on the floor next to my mother."

Matt nodded and headed toward the back door, picking up his rifle standing there.

"She's a good woman, Matt. You should marry her."

Startled, Matt swung around, but Samuel was already out of the room.

Chapter Ten

Two days later, on Second Day morning, Verity stood beside her father-in-law in the bright but chilly sunlight. Joseph was positioning old cans in a line on the fence around the small empty paddock beside their barn. The horses that had been tethered to trees nearby nickered loudly. Verity stood, wringing her hands. She was already keyed up.

Union troops would arrive in Fiddlers Grove today, the same day that she had planned to attend the meeting at Lirit Ransford's house. And now Joseph was trying to get her to use a gun. "Joseph, I didn't approve of thee bringing guns with thee." *How can I stop the violence? Where has Matthew gone this morning? Why isn't he here to meet the troops?*

"You've said that about ten times already," Joseph replied mildly. "It's good I did bring a few firearms.

And I'm going to make sure that I still can hit what I aim for. And you should, too." He walked backward, putting distance between him and the target.

He motioned for Verity to follow him. "During target practice, everyone must stay in back of the person who is firing. When I taught my boys how to handle a rifle, I was always careful about gun safety."

"Joseph, thee knows that I cannot do this. I cannot fire a weapon."

Joseph fixed her with a dark stare. "When we were attacked while raising the barn, what if Matt and Samuel hadn't had their guns? I should have had mine with me. It won't happen again. I'm not young enough to defend us with my fists. Cold steel and lead will have to make the difference."

Verity didn't know how to persuade him. "I can't do this."

"What if I'd been shot and they had tried to kill or hurt you and Beth? And I mean more than just beating her."

Verity couldn't meet his fierce eyes. She knew he was referring to rape. The idea that any man would use that kind of low, vicious violence against her, much less her sweet little daughter, made her mind go blank.

So she stood there wringing her hands. "I'm sorry, Joseph, I can't. I can't, no matter what. It is against all of my beliefs. I will have to depend on God's mercy." She hurried away, her heart still pounding at the thought of holding a gun, much less firing it.

Faithful Barney beside her, Beth awaited her on the back porch. Not surprisingly, she had been clingy and weepy ever since the attack the other day. When Verity reached her daughter, Beth put her arms around Verity's waist and hugged her as if she'd been gone for days to a foreign shore, not just a few yards away in plain sight. "Mama, I'm glad Grandpa has a gun. Is that bad?"

Verity smoothed back stray tendrils of her daughter's hair. Guilt had stalked Verity relentlessly since the attack. Did she have the right to put her father-in-law or her daughter through this? "No, it isn't bad."

"If the bad men come back, Grandpa will shoot them before they can hurt us. Won't he?"

Each question was a razor slicing into Verity's sore heart and raw conscience. *My daughter shouldn't have to ask these questions, Lord. No child should.*

Verity stroked her daughter's hair. "Beth, thy grandfather came along to protect us. He is doing what he thinks is best in order to keep us safe. But in the end, God is our shield and defender, the Ancient of Days. We must trust in God."

Beth did not look comforted by this response. *Oh, Lord, teach my child to lean upon Thee and not her own understanding.*

Verity went inside to check on her remaining two patients on pallets in the parlor. A low fire burned, warming the room. The army doctor was to come today and remove the bullets lodged too deeply for Verity to access. Verity had cleaned and rebandaged the wounds several times to keep down the infection. But the two men were weak and listless.

Hannah was helping one patient drink water. The mantel clock chimed eleven times. How would she stand the tension four more hours until she ventured out into this town that hated her? Would she be able to enlist the help of Lirit and her friends for her personal mission or would the arrival of troops put an end to that? Would the festering evil in the South kill her heartfelt hopes and prayers?

Three o'clock loomed. With feet like blocks of lead, Verity set out. She carried the precious box in her oak basket. Feeling unprepared, she arrived at Ransford Manor. Passing between the imposing Doric columns, she knocked on the broad double doors. In spite of the fact that the shiny black doors and white columns were peeling, the setting was quite impressive— and quite daunting.

Elijah answered her knock. "Good day, Miss Verity." He looked as if he wanted to ask why she'd come here today. He no longer wore a bandage but he still had a swollen eye from the skirmish over the barn raising.

She gave him a brave smile. "Good day to thee, Elijah. Mrs. Ransford has invited me to the tea."

His eyebrows rose. Finally he stepped back and she entered. The house smelled of old polished wood and candle wax. The hall had been swept and polished since her last visit. The chatter of women came from the room to the right of the staircase. Verity was certain that they couldn't be talking as loud as it sounded to her now.

"I'll tell the mistress of the house that you are here," he said in a hollow voice.

Verity's heart fluttered like a captured bird.

"That's all right, Elijah." Mrs. Ransford stood in the doorway to her parlor in a faded pink dress in the antebellum style, and wearing a gold locket at her throat. "Mrs. Hardy," the lady greeted her with a mix of hostility and mockery, "you decided to come today after all."

"Yes, I have come." Verity hoped her trembling wasn't visible.

Lirit's gaze swept over her with scorn. "Then come in and meet the Daughters of the Confederacy. They will be overcome with joy to meet you in person at last."

Ignoring the heavy sarcasm, Verity entered the parlor. Numbness started spreading through her limbs, fear freezing her. She looked from face to face. The hostile expressions on each told her that they had not expected or desired the Yankee schoolmarm to show up for tea. Verity took a deep breath and said, "Good afternoon, ladies. I have something I'd like to share with you."

A large woman with a blotchy complexion rose and snapped, "You are not welcome here. Please have the courtesy to leave."

Verity knew the moment had come. It was now or never. "I am here at Mrs. Ransford's invitation and I have something to share with all of thee—"

"Of all the nerve!" A second woman in a worn lavender dress rose and faced Verity. "We don't want to hear anymore about that Negro school you want to build here. Please leave."

"Thy hostess invited me here and I am going to stay until I've said what I came to say." Verity cast a glance at her hostess, who gloated in the parlor doorway, plainly enjoying Verity's hostile reception. Verity straightened. The time for truth-telling had come. "I'm sure that Lirit Ransford invited me here this afternoon for tea so that I would suffer public insult. But I have something of importance to tell thee—" Verity's voice gathered strength "—which has nothing to do with my Freedman's school. I'm not leaving until I have spoken to all of thee."

"Personally I cannot wait to hear what y'all have to tell us," Mrs. Ransford taunted.

Verity ignored her, though her heart skipped and thumped against her breastbone. "I do not think any of thee know that I come from Gettysburg, Pennsylvania."

Their reaction was instantaneous. The mere mention

of her hometown and the horrific battle that had cost thousands of Union and Confederate lives cast a grievous pall over the room. The large woman with the blotchy complexion slumped back into her chair.

The other woman in the lavender dress also sank down. "How can you bring that up? So many of us… How could she?" she whispered.

Verity tried to catch her breath and soften her voice. "I do not mention this to hurt anyone. But my sisters and I, along with our congregation of Friends, worked to save the lives of soldiers during that terrible battle. In the midst of all the killing, our men went out onto the battlefield and carried wounded off to our meeting house, which we set up as a hospital. My sisters, the other women of our meeting and I worked tirelessly for over two weeks trying to save lives on both sides."

Suddenly Verity couldn't go on. The appalling memories of Gettysburg made it impossible to speak for a moment. Cannon blasting, drums pounding, rifles firing; men screaming, cursing, the earth shaking under her. And blood, blood, blood everywhere. Before she disgraced herself by fainting, Verity collapsed onto the empty chair nearest her. She couldn't feel her feet, but her heart danced wildly.

The only sound was of two women weeping quietly.

"Why did you bring this up?" a woman who wore spectacles whispered. "Do you think that your nursing should impress us?"

Shaken to her core by memories, Verity was beyond being insulted. She had begun; she would finish the course. "As my sisters and I cared for the soldiers both Union and Confederate, we tried to gather their names, their hometowns and any other information we could about them. We gathered their mementos, insignia from their uniforms and pieces of identification or personal possessions. We wanted to be able to let their families know what had happened to them." Verity's throat constricted again and she tried to swallow the horrible memories of the overwhelming smell of blood and dirt and sweat. "But some of the soldiers—" she forced herself to go on "—were never able to give us their names and some no one recognized. So we put their belongings into envelopes and marked on them anything, any clues that we might have about their names and where they came from."

With numb fingers Verity fumbled open the covered oak basket that sat on her lap. She lifted out the topmost bulging envelope. "This soldier died without regaining consciousness. We found this watch." Fighting to draw breath, she held it up. "Inside the inscription reads, 'To Jesse from his loving parents.' And we found this picture in his pocket." She held up a daguerreotype of a young woman. "He wore the insignia of the South Carolina militia. And we heard him speak the name 'Louisa' several times."

"I don't understand why you are putting us through

this," said the woman in the lavender dress, who was weeping.

"I know what it feels like to lose a husband in battle. But I was fortunate enough to receive a letter from my husband's commander telling me about Roger's final days of life and how he died. The commander sent me his watch, and other personal effects. But not all women—wives, mothers, sisters, daughters—were as fortunate as I was. My sisters and I saved these precious envelopes for after the war. We did this in hopes that we would be able to find the women, the families to whom these keepsakes would mean so much. But we are at a loss with regards to finding these people." Verity felt a headache begin behind her eyes.

"What you expect us to do?" the large woman asked, no longer sounding hostile but now only quietly distressed.

"I am hoping that thee, all of thee, will take on the task of finding the families of these men as a work of charity. I know that thee all have relatives and friends all over the South and can also contact people who fought with thy husbands. I'm hoping—my sisters and I are hoping—that thee will be able to return these mementos to the rightful heirs."

There was again silence, except for the weeping. Then Verity felt tears dripping down her face. She hadn't even realized she'd been crying. She found her handkerchief and wiped her face. "Will thee accept this work of charity?"

From outside came the sound of horses. Lirit moved to the window. "Yankee troops have come," she said in a flat tone. "Matt Ritter's riding with them. We should have known that he'd come back and take revenge on us."

Verity tensed, feeling the progress she'd made with the women slipping away. *Dear Father, please, no.*

Late that afternoon in the chill early darkness, Verity walked the last few steps to her house. Feeling a hundred years older than she had this morning, she saw that their paddock was occupied by several strange horses. She trudged up the steps and inside, hearing male voices in the parlor where the last few wounded lay. She took off her bonnet and hung it on the hall tree. After the emotional scene at the tea, Verity felt worn out. And now she must face Union troops, an army doctor and Matthew. She clearly understood why Matthew had to summon these troops. But was there any way she could avoid a local backlash?

She moved into the parlor, her head aching. The army doctor was kneeling beside one of the patients, examining an open wound on the patient's shoulder. Unfortunately, this sight no longer had the power to shock her.

Matthew was standing nearby. At sight of him—his

dark good looks—her heart sped up. She tried to temper this reaction, but it was in vain. "You went to meet
the troops?" she asked, trying to ignore the unseen pull
toward him.

"No, I went to Richmond to swear out a warrant for
Orrin Dyke's arrest," Matthew said, not meeting her
eyes.

"His arrest?" She folded her arms around herself
and tried to smooth back her unruly hair.

"Yes. Isn't that what you'd expect? He attacked
me, set fire to the house and threatened to kill you. All
of those are punishable felonies."

Her hair was straying from her sagging bun, and
she was pushing in her loose hairpins. When she realized she was doing this for Matthew, she lowered her
arms and cleared her throat. "Thee is right, of course.
Orrin Dyke broke the law." It was odd how her mind
had become muddled here, as if the normal rules of
crime and punishment were still suspended by the
war.

"A few of the soldiers came back with me and they've
gone on to arrest Dyke at his house," Matthew said.

Fighting her desire to gaze at Matthew, she nodded.
It would be a relief to have Orrin Dyke behind bars.
She wanted to tell Matthew what she'd done today, but
she suspected that he wouldn't be pleased. It was
strange how they always seemed to be at odds, even
though they were on the same side.

Now she knew from what Samuel had said the other night that Matthew's family had been driven out of Fiddlers Grove because they had been abolitionists. This must have been what had caused the bad feelings between Dace and Matthew, and it was understandable. Terribly sad, but understandable.

The army doctor rose and bowed to her. "You are a fine nurse, ma'am. I only need extract the balls from these men and they will be on the mend."

"Thank thee," Verity replied. "My sister Mercy worked with Clara Barton throughout the war. On her few furloughs, she taught us to treat war wounds."

"Women like your sister did so much for us doctors." He moved to shake her hand. "Please offer my compliments to her."

Verity shook his hand and smiled.

"Ritter, why don't you take Mrs. Hardy outside?" the doctor said. "I'm sure that this woman here is capable of assisting me." He nodded toward Hannah.

The doctor had just complimented her on her nursing skills, but he still thought a "lady" shouldn't be present at surgery. She hid a wry smile, allowing Matthew to lead her into the kitchen, a hazardous venture. She steeled herself, knowing she must not let his effect on her show. It would be embarrassing for both of them.

This was the first time they'd been alone for days. She waved him to take a seat. The kitchen smelled of roast beef and onions—Hannah must have their supper in the oven. She went to the stove to see if there was any coffee left to put off sitting across from him. There wasn't any so she prepared the percolator for more and stoked the fire under the pot. She found her traitorous eyes gazing at his profile, admiring his straight nose and firm chin.

"I thought I asked you not to go off alone," Matthew scolded.

"I don't remember thee saying that." She clutched two faded blue potholders in her hands.

"I did. Where did you go?" He looked her in the eye.

She avoided his gaze and moved to the dry sink, refolding a couple of kitchen towels there. Again, the time had come for honesty. She took a deep steadying breath. "I went to Ransford Manor to attend the Daughters of the Confederacy meeting that Lirit invited me to on Thanksgiving."

"You what?" He stood up, scraping the wood floor with the chair legs.

She lifted her chin and held her ground. "Thee heard me, Matthew."

"Are you a glutton for punishment?" He looked at her as if she were completely deranged. "Wasn't the Thanksgiving debacle enough for you?"

"I had something I had to do." She went to the table and sat down, her knees weak with the memory of walking into that den of lionesses with Lirit Ransford sneering at her.

Not taking his eyes from hers, he sat back down across from her.

She tried not to stare into his dark eyes, nor at the cleft in his chin that beckoned her to press her finger to it.

"What was so important that you went out alone and unprotected when Orrin Dyke was still at large?"

"I had to try to reach them, to appeal to them. I came here to teach school, but I have another mission to carry out, Matthew." The coffeepot was beginning to rumble, simmering.

"What mission?" His arm was on the red-and-white-checked oilcloth, his hand just inches from hers.

Its nearness made her own hand unnaturally sensitive, as if already feeling his skin against hers. "My family's Friends Meeting House was used as a field hospital and my sisters and I nursed wounded during and after the battle of Gettysburg." She passed a hand over her forehead. "You know how dreadful that was," she appealed to him, a shiver coursing through her. "So many died without telling us who they were and where they were from. My sisters and I gathered mementoes from their uniforms and pockets, keeping them in separate envelopes. I brought them with me to Virginia."

His hand clasped hers, sending warmth through her. His voice was low and rough. "I don't understand what you thought the women in Fiddlers Grove could do with them."

Despite his words, she glimpsed understanding in his eyes. "They have relatives and friends all over the South." Her voice lifted, filled with passion and the hope of comforting others who had lost beloved men just as she had. "They can begin the work of getting the mementoes to the loved ones who would so long for them. It may take years but…I hope they will take on this work of charity. It would mean so much to those left behind."

He stared at her and said nothing. His thumb gently stroked her palm. They listened to the coffeepot bubbling on the cast-iron burner.

She finally broke the silence. "I had to try, Matthew. Thee sees that, doesn't thee?"

"Did they stone you or just tell you to get out?"

The bitterness in his voice stabbed her. She tightened her hold on his hand as if it were a lifeline. *Oh, Matthew, when will thy hurt be healed?* "The ladies looked stunned at first. Just the mention of Gettysburg shook them. I left the box of mementos with them and I hope they will take on this task. It has been a burden on my heart."

He wouldn't look at her, but he didn't withdraw his hand. "You're too good for this time, this place."

"I am not good, Matthew. Only God is good."

"No, you are good." He drew her hand to his lips and placed one brief, tender kiss there.

Verity closed her eyes, her every sense focused on

the spot his lips had touched. *Please, Matthew, tread lightly. Caring for each other is not to be. Not here. Not now.* But she had to fight herself to keep from pressing her hand to her cheek. The percolator was nearly boiling over. She leaped up to take it from the burner. *Oh, Matthew, I can't care for you.*

The next day Matt stood in the yard where the new barn would rise in a matter of hours. His spine was straight and his jaw was like iron. The local men who were able to work stood around the barn site with a dozen soldiers who were meant to stay until both the barn and school were built. The soldiers had decided to help, since sitting around in the chilly wind didn't agree with them. Plus the sooner the buildings were up, the sooner they could get back to Richmond.

So let trouble come, Matt thought as he walked toward them. If anyone tried to stop them today, they'd end up in the Richmond Union stockade for a very long time.

This wouldn't be a normal, festive barn raising. Verity and Hannah were still tending the wounded in the parlor. The food prepared on Friday had been given away, so the men had brought their own food with them in pails. And they'd left their women at home.

The men still bore swollen bruises and half-healed cuts from the last skirmish in this yard. Matt still ached from Orrin's fists. And they all kept looking over their shoulders as if expecting those against them to come and start fighting all over again—in spite of the presence of Union troops.

Matt was pleased that for once, Verity had listened to him and agreed to stay inside along with Hannah and Beth. Alec was still laid up, but soon he'd be able to go home on his own. Orrin Dyke had run for it and was still at large, but now with a price on his head. Perhaps luck would be on their side this time. Matt looked around and shouted, "Let's get started!"

"Let's pray," Joseph suggested.

Matt prickled with irritation, but the men around him looked relieved. He bowed his head with them but looked up instantly at the sound of a horse approaching. His cousin was riding toward the back door as cool as can be. *I'm ready for you, Dace.* Matt's hands balled into fists.

But Dace merely halted and tethered his horse to the back porch railing. He waved at Matt and then sat down on the top porch step.

Matt stared hard, not knowing what to make of Dace's appearance. Then he turned, calling, "Let's get this barn up!" Hammers and saws sounded in the quiet morning. The men began singing "Down by the Riverside."

When Matt looked up again, he saw that the vicar of St. John's had come, too, and was leaning against the railing, talking to Dace. And then the preacher from the community church—the one who'd ordered them to leave—sauntered up and joined them. The men around him kept working, but they stopped singing. Matt felt their keen watchfulness, matched by his own heightened sense of perception.

Then Jed McKay, Mary Dyke's father, rode up on an old nag, followed closely by Mary in a buckboard. "I can't believe my eyes! Have you three gone plumb crazy?"

"Pa—" she said.

"Be silent, girl! Women are not to speak in public. Says so in the Good Book. Preacher," McKay said, glaring at his pastor, "why are you here? You ain't got anything better to do?"

"I'm here to make sure no violence is done today. We may not like this school, but I don't want Union troops in Fiddlers Grove any longer than necessary."

"Yes," the vicar agreed, "the school is going to happen with or without us. Why fight it?"

"Fight it? I'll fight it with my last breath!" McKay bellowed.

Matt saw Verity just outside the back door. The two clergymen and Dace rose and tipped their hats at her. *Stay there, Verity.* Matt didn't want her drawing fire. Readiness for battle set his nerves on edge.

McKay shook his fist. "The U.S. Congress rammed the Thirteenth Amendment through before the South could do anything about it. So the slaves are free. But are y'all in favor of the Fourteenth Amendment? Do you really want blacks to be full citizens? Like white people?" McKay demanded.

"Thee cannot hold back the future," Verity insisted. "And what is wrong with letting children in this town learn to read?"

McKay pointed a finger at her without looking her way. "Orrin Dyke was the only one in town that was willing to stand up to this Yankee schoolmarm. And y'all let her run him out of town! Can't you people see that she's just not like us?"

"Orrin started a fire in the house," Matt yelled. "Attacked Mrs. Hardy and me, Jed McKay." He closed the distance between them. "He's a wanted man. That's why he's run away! He's a coward. Is that what you call a *good* man?" Matt let all his disdain flow in each word.

To Matt's surprise, Dace said, "The barn and the school are going up. Go home, McKay."

Jed turned on Dace. "What I want to know, Ransford, is why you've been in her pocket since she came to town. If you'd just taken a strong stand against this woman, the men in this town would have rallied behind you like they did when you got up our company to fight. Why have you tolerated this? In fact, you've encouraged her. You even sat at table with her!"

"The answer is quite simple," Dace replied. "She saved my life."

Jed McKay stared at him, openmouthed. The men

in the yard turned toward Dace and then gawked at Mrs. Hardy.

"What does thee mean?" Verity asked, sounding shocked.

Matt tried to make sense of Dace's words. Dace couldn't be serious.

"Mrs. Hardy," Dace said, holding out his hand, "I have not wanted to tell you because I thought it might make you feel uncomfortable. But I was one of those sad men you nursed in your Quaker meeting house during the Battle of Gettysburg."

Verity gasped and her hand went to her throat in surprise. "Thee?" Tears welled up in her eyes.

Matt tried to grasp this—Verity nursed Dace?

"Yes. At first I wasn't sure that it had been you, but after my first visit, I knew. I could not mistake your lovely caring voice. It was life to me one very long, pain-filled night." Dace's voice sank and became rougher.

"I—I'm sorry I didn't recognize thee," Verity stammered, taking Dace's hand.

"How could you? I was one of hundreds. But I remember lying there and hearing the doctor tell you that I needed very careful nursing through the night or I'd die. And you stayed with me, bathing my face and cleaning my wound over and over. I'm sure if you hadn't, I would have died that night. I was too weak even to ask your name or to thank you."

"I'm glad I could help you," she said.

Dace's words brought back harsh memories forever etched on Matt's mind and heart. He wiped his eyes with the heels of his hands.

Jed McKay cursed loud and long. "What does it matter? She is bringing wrong ideas into this town! You give blacks school-learning and the next they'll want is the vote. Haven't you read about the riots in Louisiana and Tennessee? The Negroes there demanded the vote! You mark my words—you'll have blacks voting and running for Congress in Virginia if we don't put a stop to this right now!"

Matt stood straighter. "You're right, McKay. And the sooner the better."

A stunned silence filled the yard. McKay glared, red-faced and white-lipped. "We don't want or need Yankee schoolmarms teaching blacks to be 'colored gentlemen.'" He made the terms sound like vile insults as he dismounted. "We can keep blacks in their place in this town if you stand with me today and run this Quaker and Matthew Ritter out of town! Who stands with me? Who stands for what is right?"

The troops almost casually reached for their rifles and turned them on McKay and the other two whites. The black men brandished their tools as weapons, ready for anything.

Then Samuel stepped forward. "Any man that can

be happy to have his daughter married to a brute like Orrin Dyke is a man I can disagree with—cheerfully."

"You've got that right," Matt seconded.

"No one asked you to open your mouth, boy!" McKay roared. He charged Samuel. Dace leaped forward and grabbed Jed's arms. The old man struggled against him.

"Orrin *is* a brute." Mary Dyke's thin, frightened voice shocked everyone into silence. "I told my father that Orrin beat me and he told me to mind my man and I wouldn't be ill-treated. He was wrong. Orrin didn't need a reason to hurt me and my son." Mary's voice shook with feeling. "I'm glad Orrin's gone. I hope he stays gone."

"You dare to speak against your husband in public?" McKay demanded.

"I dare because of this woman." Mary nodded toward Verity. "I didn't think women could make a difference, or could stand up to men. But she did. She stood up to the women, too, and showed them what she was about. I didn't know a woman could do that. If Mrs. Hardy can stand up to all of you, so can I."

Then Jed yanked himself free of Dace's grasp, mounted his horse and rode away without a backward glance. All eyes watched him until he disappeared from sight.

Mary approached Verity, the men giving way to her. "I've come to take my boy home, ma'am. Thank you for giving him shelter. I knew he was safe with you. May I see him please?"

"Of course." Verity motioned Mary up the steps and took her inside.

McKay should be horsewhipped for letting Orrin abuse his daughter and grandson. After a quick glance at his cousin, Matt turned away, choked up. "Show's over! Let's get moving! The sun goes down early these days."

Matt felt good, really good. If nothing else, he'd come home and had run Orrin out of Mary's life. With Verity's help.

The long, eventful day was finally finished. Matt thought it might take him a long time to sort through his reactions to all that had happened today. He ached, but in a good way and for a good reason. The barn was up and only needed some finishing work, which Joseph had offered to do so the men could move right on to the school tomorrow. The workers had all gone home with pay vouchers and smiles. Now sitting at the kitchen table, Matt wrote out the last voucher to Samuel.

Samuel looked at it and smiled. "Matt, when we were boys, did you ever think that you'd be paying me—a free man—for building a school for black children and former slaves in Fiddlers Grove?"

Matt was caught up short. He hadn't thought of it

in that way. "My parents hoped for, worked for something like that."

Samuel's face sobered. "They were good folk. I'm sorry they didn't live to see this day. To witness this miracle."

"This was a day of miracles," Verity said, walking into the kitchen.

Samuel rose. "Time I left for home. Good evening, Mrs. Hardy."

Matt had also risen at her entry. As Samuel passed through the back door, he winked at Matt.

Matt felt himself warm under the collar.

"Would thee like to take a walk, Matthew?" Verity asked. "I feel the need of some fresh air to clear my head. So much has happened this day."

He nodded. "Good idea." The truth was, he wanted Verity to himself. The house was crowded with soldiers bedding down in the parlor, the dining room and the entry hall. Verity had insisted they sleep inside because of the cold.

She tied her bonnet ribbons and Matt helped her on with her cape. He was careful not to touch her shoulders. Touching her might unleash all he fought to conceal. He shrugged on his wool jacket and they stepped outside into the cloaking darkness of early December.

The moon was high and bright as Matt walked beside Verity. He listened to everything with new ears, it seemed. Their footsteps sounded loud in the quiet. Matt was very aware of the woman who walked beside him, the rustling of her starched skirt. Though he longed to claim her hands, he kept his arms at his sides.

Finally she broke their silence. She did not turn toward him. "Thee doesn't believe in miracles then?"

He was about to say he didn't—then he recalled all he'd witnessed today. "I haven't for a long time," he said finally. "Is it a miracle or coincidence that Dace was one of the many you nursed at Gettysburg?"

"I call it Providence."

"Providence?" Matt asked, and shoved his chilled hands into his pockets.

"Yes. Surely my reunion with thy cousin is no mere coincidence. I don't believe in coincidence. Far in advance, God knew that I would come to Fiddlers Grove to open this school for freed slaves."

Leaves were falling in cascades from tree branches, sounding like sighs and whispers. Once again Matt wished Verity wouldn't wear such a deep-brimmed bonnet. He wanted to watch her vivid expressions. For a woman who radiated peace, she felt and showed everything vibrantly. "You believe that God had this all planned?" he asked, knowing what her reply would be.

An owl hooted in the moonlit darkness. "I do. God saved Dacian's life that awful night, not my poor nursing. He saved thy cousin for this purpose. And God preserved thy life, too. Thee is a part of this, a part of God's foreknowledge and providence."

Her voice grew stronger, with the passion that he loved in her. And hated. *Don't care so much, Verity. That's the way to pain. I'm afraid for you.* He turned his collar up against the cold.

"I don't know," he hedged. "It all sounds wonderful when you say it like that. As if God has a grand plan with parts for each of us to play—"

"It's the war, isn't it?" she interrupted. "The war cost thee much."

"I don't want to talk about it," Matt insisted, suddenly flushed. He didn't want to go back to those years, a collection of days no living soul should have had to face. "I won't."

"As thee wishes. I'm sorry. I remember…" Her voice trailed off.

She sparked his anger. He stopped her and gripped her slender shoulders. Her face shone pale in the moonlight. "You only survived one battle," Matt growled, "and you weren't in the midst of it all…" How could she know what it had been like, having to face over and over the possibility of pain, dismemberment and perhaps anonymous death.

He thought of the prebattle ritual of writing his name and town on a slip of paper and having a friend pin it to his collar. That way, if he fell, he wouldn't die nameless. The men from whom Verity had collected belongings must not have done this. Or their slips of paper had gotten torn off or lost. *God, no one should ever have to do that. No one.*

A gust of wind billowed her dark skirt. "I know. I don't know how thee did what thee did, survived what thee survived. But I know enough to know that it cost thee much, too much. And through it all, thee remained a good man, a kind man. How did thee manage that?"

He heard the sorrow and compassion in her voice, and he could hold off no longer. He pulled her into his arms. "Just put it behind you. Just say it's over."

"But it isn't over."

He didn't ask her what she meant. He drank in the sensation of her breathing against him, of her bonnet touching his face. He pressed his cheek to her forehead, wishing she were wrong. But she was right—it wasn't over. The school wasn't built and Orrin Dyke was on the loose. The hate just went on.

Chapter Eleven

It was a week later on the morning of Second Day. This would be the very first day that class would be held in the new school. Verity couldn't recall ever feeling quite this happy or uplifted. Halfway between their house and the school, she and Beth walked hand in hand through the windbreak of poplars. The morning air was crisp and clear. Behind them, smoke from the chimney puffed high and white in the blue sky, following them. For the first time in her life, Verity felt like singing out loud, hearing her own voice. Then she laughed at the silly thought. *I don't even know if I can carry a tune.*

Beth, who had finally conceded and left her dog at home with Hannah, looked up. "Mama, is this going to be a good day?"

The worry in her daughter's strained eyes pierced

Verity. She halted and pulled Beth into a tight hug. "Dearest daughter, today will be a very good day. We open the school today. The children in Fiddlers Grove will be able to learn to read and write."

"But only the black children, right? Alec won't get to learn." Beth's dismay over this darkened her deep brown eyes. Even Beth's voice drooped.

Her happiness dimming, Verity looked over the top of Beth's bonnet. *Father, I thank Thee that my daughter has a tender heart.* "Beth, whether Alec learns or not isn't up to me. But I wouldn't stop any child from coming to school—ever." *Maybe, Lord, Mary would let him come over to the house and I could teach him his letters at the kitchen table.*

Beth tugged at Verity's arm. "So if Alec came to school today, you'd let him stay?"

Verity bent, kissed Beth's forehead and cupped her chin. "Of course." But Alec wouldn't be coming to school today. The whites here had made it clear they would have nothing to do with the Freedman's school—even though that meant their own children would remain illiterate. Verity drew Beth along with her. *There are none so blind as those who will not see.*

The new white one-room school loomed ahead of them. The frozen grass under their feet crunched. On Seventh Day, the desks and blackboard had arrived and had been installed the same day. It had taken only four days for the willing workers, with the soldiers' help, to put up the school, paint it and then outfit it.

At twilight yesterday, Verity had walked down the center aisle and placed a large, leather-bound dictionary on her desk. Then she'd laid her hands on the two stacks of textbooks there—one a reader and one a math book. *It will be so good to be in the classroom once more.*

The bubbly feeling came again. Then ahead she saw the children and their mothers, bundled up against the cold and waiting outside the school door. Thaddeus Ellington Ransford ran toward them. "Schoolteacher! Schoolteacher! Now we got us a real school. Does it got chairs?"

Verity couldn't help herself. She chuckled. "Yes, yes! We have desks with chairs."

"Mama!" Beth shouted, pointing ahead. "It's Alec! Alec, did you come to school today?" Beth broke away from Verity and ran to her friend.

Alec still wore the sling, but he was walking now. His mother was standing behind him, looking uncomfortable but determined. "Good morning, Mrs. Hardy."

"Good morning, Mary." Verity looked around. There seemed to be two camps—one on each side of the door. The black mothers and children stood to the left, and a few white mothers and children to the right. Verity's spirits dropped to her toes. Would there be a confrontation on this bright, promising day? *Father, help.*

"Mrs. Hardy, I know this school is just for freed slaves and their children, but Alec wanted to come. He wants to learn…" Mary said, her frail voice fading away.

"Don't worry, ma'am." Beth spoke up with palpable confidence. "My mama won't turn away anyone who wants to learn. She told me so." Beth gave Alec a look of delight and danced on her toes. "You can learn, too, Alec. Reading is fun!"

Verity glanced at the black mothers, who looked skeptical. *This must come from thee, Lord. I couldn't have caused it.* She decided the best course of action was just to go on as if this unexpected turn hadn't occurred. *Please, Lord, keep care of this. It's beyond me.*

She walked to the door and unlocked it. Earlier this morning, Joseph had come over and started a fire in the Franklin stove in the center of the school, so the school was pristine, welcoming and warm. "Come in! Come in! Hang your coats on the hooks on the back wall. Those children who have already been registered and attending school, take your seats according to your age as you did on the porch."

The black children scrambled to take their seats, all the while exclaiming over the brand-new desks. Alec hung back, but Beth dragged him forward by the hand. "Alec, you're a boy so you sit on this side. And you're bigger, so you sit back here."

The black mothers had gone forward to examine

Verity's desk. The white mothers—Mary and, to Verity's surprise, two women whom Verity had seen at the Daughters of the Confederacy meeting—walked in hesitantly, looking all around. They motioned their children to sit in the back behind the black children.

Before Verity could say anything, Sassy Ellington Ransford stood up and waved to them. "You white chil'run got to come up to the teacher and tell her your name—all your names. If you ain't got three, she'll give you what you need." Sassy waved again, summoning them forward. "Come on. She got to write your names in the book so she can mark down when you come every day. It's called taking roll."

The white children followed their mothers and moved forward, looking as if they'd been transported to China and couldn't believe their eyes or ears. Trying not to laugh at Sassy's instructions, Verity took off her cape and bonnet, and hung them on a hook on the wall nearby. Then she sat at her desk and opened her roll book and inkwell. With her pen in hand, she said, "Tell me your full names, please, one at a time."

She enrolled three white boys including Alec, and one white girl—Annie, the granddaughter of the large woman with the blotchy complexion who'd ordered her out of Lirit's parlor. The woman, Mrs. Augusta Colbert, gave Verity an intense look. "We're trusting you to know how to do this."

Do what? Teach? Integrate a school? Verity tried

not to appear as baffled as she felt and merely nodded, trying to look confident.

With that, the mothers departed, leaving Verity facing the children. The black children sat in the front rows and the new white students sat behind them. Beth had taken her accustomed seat near Sassy. All the children looked eager and uncertain. The mixing of the two races—something that Verity had never expected—seemed to put everyone on edge. Except for Sassy.

Verity took a deep breath and began calling roll, name by name. Each of the experienced students stood and replied to her, and then sat back down. Sassy turned and alerted the white children in a stage whisper that they should do that, too. So when Verity called, "Alec Jedediah Dyke," Alec rose and replied, "Present, ma'am." Then, as if he couldn't help it, Alec grinned—it was the first smile she'd ever seen on his face. Verity blinked away the moisture gathering in her eyes. *I thank Thee, Father, for this moment. It gives me hope.*

After roll, Verity began the daily alphabet instruction. The experienced students recited with enthusiasm while the new ones only observed. It would probably take some time for them to become comfortable enough to join in.

As Verity was about to finish the first math lesson, Matthew and Samuel came through the door. Her heart skittered in her chest. *Oh, no, what's wrong now?*

"Good morning, Mrs. Hardy!" Samuel called out with a smile. "Good morning, students!" He stopped short when he caught sight of the white students. Matthew halted beside him, looking uncomfortable.

Oh, dear. She'd surprised him again. And he didn't look pleased. Verity drew in a breath and forced a smile.

"Hello, Mr. Ritter," Alec said. "And you, too, Samuel."

Recovering quickly, Samuel waved to Alec and the other children. Matthew nodded at them, still looking perplexed by the white children at the back.

"What may we do for thee today, gentlemen?" Verity asked, hoping to forestall any questions about the additions to her classroom.

"Well…I…" Samuel said. "We thought that this new school needed some decorating." He looked around, grinning. "I mean, it's almost Christmas! When I went to school in the North, we always had a tree and pine branches on the windowsills. And I thought that Fiddlers Grove's first school needed them, too." Samuel put an arm around Matthew's shoulders. "And Matt here agreed with me."

A sudden lightness rose inside her. She smothered a chuckle. She could just imagine how enthusiastic Matthew had been about this idea. "Well, what do you think, children? Should our new school be decorated for Christmas?"

Beth jumped up, waving her hand. "Yes, Mama—I mean, yes, ma'am!"

Bouncing on her toes, Sassy had joined Beth and actually had to put both hands over her mouth to keep from speaking without waiting for permission.

"Sassy?" Verity said.

The little girl waved her hand like a flag. "Please, ma'am, we want to decorate our school! We never had a Christmas tree like they did in the big house!"

"Then I think that first the girls and then the boys should line up and put on thy coats and scarves. Then form a line and wait for permission to go outside. Thee will not run and thee will stay close to me." Verity pointed toward the aisle and the coatrack. The girls lined up and soon all the children stood in two lines, waiting to head outside.

Matthew found his voice. "We left the hatchets outside and we have a wooded section at the back of this property with pines and holly trees on it. I thought we'd cut one for the school and one for the house," Matt said.

"Wonderful." Verity beamed at him, tugging on her gloves.

A warmth glowed inside him to see her so happy after all she'd gone through over the past weeks. He smiled as he helped her with her cape.

"Will thee two gentlemen lead us then?" At his nod, she said, "Children, please follow Matthew and Samuel."

Samuel stayed at the head of the party, encouraging the children with teasing. The children's zest was contagious—Matt felt his mood lifting. As they tromped over the frozen grass, he drifted back to Verity's side, bringing up the rear.

The clear, cold air was invigorating and he breathed it in deeply, trying to shake off his powerful attraction to this woman. He leaned close to her, wishing her bonnet away. Its brim hid her face from him. He whispered, "How did the white children come to be in the school? Did you do something?" *And not tell me as usual?*

She tilted her head so he could see her face, framed by the brim. "I arrived at school and there they were with their mothers. I was taken completely by surprise. But I'm not sorry. I hope more white children will come."

What would the Freedman's Bureau have to say about white children in this school? Well, that would have to take care of itself. He wasn't going to tell Verity Hardy that she couldn't let white children into her classroom. He wasn't crazy.

"What kind of tree do you children think we should have in your school?" Samuel called out.

"A big one!" Thaddeus shouted.

"The biggest one!" Sassy seconded.

Verity chuckled and Matthew felt laughter rolling around in him. He finally let it come up his throat. He laughed out loud. "The biggest one?" he called out. "We'd better not get one so tall that we have to cut a hole in the roof."

The children giggled at this. And Verity touched his arm. He looked down and she was beaming at him again. Making him forget they were colleagues. Making him want more, much more from her.

Soon they reached the wooded area. There were white pines, yellow pines, spruce trees, cedar trees. The children scrambled around, shouting about each tree they deemed a possible choice.

Matthew now realized how much all the opposition from the town had affected him. Each moment of listening to the children, listening to Samuel teasing them, lifted him and seemed to chip away at the burden he'd carried not for weeks but for years. He found himself keeping close to Verity, as if she were his North Star, glowing and leading him away from…what?

He couldn't put it into words. It just felt good. Just being near her, hearing her soft voice and her chuckling. Over and over, she turned her face up to him, beaming, shining, happy. Her enjoyment infused him, too.

Right here, right now it was hard to recall that Orrin Dyke was still at large. And that many in Fiddlers Grove would be outraged that white children had attended school with black children, and that together they were running around in the woods, choosing a Christmas tree.

Then he felt it—an icy dot melting on his face. He looked up. Snowflakes were drifting down. The children squealed with delight. "Snow! Snow!" they called out. "It's snowing!"

"God is blessing us," Verity murmured, her face skyward, her eyes shut.

And Matt leaned down and brushed her lips with his. Verity's eyes opened wide. Heart racing, Matt turned from her, calling, "Who's found the tallest tree?"

Over the next few weeks, Verity wondered if she'd imagined Matthew's lips brushing hers. But every time she looked around her classroom, she was reminded of the day they'd gone together to cut the Christmas tree for the school, and she knew it wasn't her imagination.

Christmas Eve had finally come. And she would be taking another chance, making another attempt to break down the barriers in the town.

At the front of the dimly lit classroom, the yellow pine tree they'd cut stood, lovingly decorated with strings of popcorn, sprigs of holly with red berries, pinecones painted white and white candles clipped to a few branches. And adorning each windowsill was a single candle in a glass globe set on pine boughs with bright red holly berries and shiny green holly leaves. Matthew's kiss remained as real as these solid reminders of the day he'd kissed her.

His kiss had been like the touch of an angel's wing or what she imagined an angel's wing would feel like—light and fleeting, just like the snowflakes that had been falling that day. *Matthew Ritter did kiss me.*

And he will be vexed with me again. Matthew had been called to Richmond four days ago for meetings about starting the Union League of America the day after Christmas. And while he was gone, she'd made another decision that he probably wouldn't like.

"Schoolteacher, we done making the school look like a barn," Sassy announced to Verity, bringing her back to the hubbub of her classroom. Outside the windows the sky was dark. Only the moonlight through the windows, the candles and one oil lamp at the front illuminated the shadowy classroom. The Franklin stove warmed the room. Verity's heart was skipping, worry and anticipation making themselves felt.

Verity glanced down at Sassy's bright eyes and full smile, cupping the little girl's cheek. She then checked the room to see that everything was in place. Her desk had been moved to the rear beside the door. And where it usually stood was a manger with hay and various tackle that one would find in a barn—hay bales, rakes, harnesses, a sawhorse. They brought with them the earthy scent of livestock and wood.

"School look different at night," Sassy said in a lower and softer voice than usual, with a note of wonder in it.

"Yes, it does. It looked like this the night Jesus was

born in Bethlehem." Each boy had a dish cloth tied around his head as the only costume. The girls wore white ribbons around their heads as halos. Verity had tried to enlist a few boy angels, but the universal sentiment from Fiddlers Grove boys—regardless of color—was that angels could be played only by girls. She had bowed to their preference.

"Did He have a Christmas tree?" Thaddeus asked, sidling up to her. Like most children, he had an insatiable urge to be touched, to be loved. Verity squeezed his shoulder.

"No, Jesus didn't have a tree," Alec said, standing in the center aisle, his voice kind to the younger boy. "It was in olden times. They didn't do Christmas trees, remember? Teacher told us about it."

Verity couldn't believe the change in Alec. A few weeks of coming to school and being recognized as an excellent student had made such a change to him. The image of the first time she'd seen Alec battered and bruised flashed in her mind. She swallowed down the harsh memory, nerves clenching inside.

"Oh, I forgot Jesus didn't have a Christmas tree," Thaddeus admitted, hanging his head.

Verity squeezed the boy's shoulder again. "Thee will remember next time."

Thaddeus beamed at her.

"Mama," Beth said with a smile that spread over her face, "I hear people coming!"

Verity was certain that she'd heard voices outside for the past few minutes. She looked at her students. "Now, we've all practiced this a good long time." *The past three days.* "The only thing that will be different is that Mr. Ransford will be doing the reading, not me." Another decision Matthew probably wouldn't like.

The thought of having Fiddlers Grove's most important citizen come to take part in this production with them seemed to ignite a special excitement that raced through the children. Sassy and Beth weren't the only girls dancing and clapping.

"Now get back behind the curtain and I'll let everyone in," Verity said, herding them all behind a large white bedsheet that she and Hannah had hung right after school today. Joseph was already there to help keep peace.

Then she took a deep breath and opened wide the school door. "Come in!" she invited, alive in the moment. "Welcome! Merry Christmas!"

Dacian Ransford was first at the doorway. He let his obviously truculent wife precede him. He bowed over Verity's hand and she showed him to the front of the classroom, where a Bible and a lamp sat on a desk to the right. Lirit sat down in the rear, as far as possible from her husband. Then the black parents streamed in, followed by Joseph.

Verity noticed that everyone had dressed up for the

occasion and she was glad she'd worn her best black. A few white parents sifted in and arranged themselves near the back of the room as if they didn't want to be noticed.

The little school was soon packed. Mothers and teenagers sat in the desks while the men stood around the perimeter of the room, holding their hats in front of them. Verity noticed that in the rear the curtain was billowing and she detected the telltale movement of pushing and shoving. But before she could get there, Hannah had gone behind the curtain to help Joseph and was giving the children a stiff lecture in a low but stern voice.

Verity had planned this event for six in the evening as most of the children were little and needed to get home for early bedtimes. Noting that it was time to get started, she walked up the center aisle. When she turned to look out over the assembly, everyone fell silent.

Speaking in front of so many strangers gave Verity the jitters. Their faces flickered in front of her eyes, but she persevered. "I'm so happy that thee were able to come this evening to our first Christmas play. I hope it will be the first of many. Elijah, would thee please offer a prayer for us?"

Standing, Elijah cleared his throat and asked for God's blessing, thanking him for Jesus's birth. When everyone lifted their heads again, Verity said, "Now the children of Fiddlers Grove's first school will enact the Christmas story for thy enjoyment and blessing. Dacian, will thee begin reading, please?"

Verity walked swiftly to the rear, where the oldest students in the class, Alec and Beth, waited to start. *Lord, bless this hour to Thy glory.*

Lifting the open Bible beside the oil lamp, Dacian began, "I am reading from the Gospel of Luke, chapter two.

"And it came to pass in those days, that there went out a decree from Caesar Augustus that all the world should be taxed. (And this taxing was first made when Cyrenius was governor of Syria.) And all went to be taxed, every one into his own city."

Verity motioned Alec and Beth to begin slowly walking down the center aisle, Alec supporting Beth on his arm. A rustle of excitement rippled through the crowd as every head turned to watch. Verity had let the students vote who would make the best Mary and Joseph, and these two had been the unanimous choice.

"And Joseph also went up from Galilee, out of the city of Nazareth, into Judaea, unto the city of David, which is called Bethlehem; (because he was of the house and lineage of David:) To be taxed with Mary his espoused wife, being great with child. And so it was, that, while they were there, the days were accomplished that she should be delivered. And she brought forth her firstborn son, and wrapped him in swaddling clothes, and laid him in a manger; because there was no room for them in the inn."

At this point Alec lifted a sheet in front of Beth. When he lowered it, Beth was holding a rag doll swaddled in a white blanket. Quickly, Verity sent Sassy and Annie up the aisle, leading all the other girls with their white-ribbon halos.

When they were halfway up the aisle, Verity sent five boys with canes held like shepherds' staffs after them. She wished Matthew were here to see the joy on the children's faces. Then he might not disapprove of this quite as much. She drew in more air, holding down her churning tension.

"And there were in the same country shepherds abiding in the field, keeping watch over their flock by night. And, lo, the angel of the Lord came upon them, and the glory of the Lord shone round about them: and they were sore afraid."

Halfway up the aisle, the shepherds dropped to their knees, the canes clattering to the wood floor. Sassy, the angel, motioned broadly with her hand.

"And the angel said unto them…"

Sassy and Annie shouted, "Fear not!" Verity had been certain that Sassy couldn't keep quiet the whole time and had taken the precaution of giving her a line. She was so proud of her students she didn't notice the classroom door open.

Matt and Samuel slipped inside the warm and darkened classroom, closing the door silently behind them. Verity did not look up. She appeared to be concentrating intensely as Dace read from the Bible.

Matt wasn't prepared for his reaction to seeing Verity after several days away from her. Awareness of her flashed through him like a summer wind. Without Verity's presence, Richmond had felt sterile and lacking.

Dace glanced toward the little angels and, grinning, continued.

"For, behold, I bring you good tidings of great joy, which shall be to all people. For unto you is born this day in the city of David a Saviour, which is Christ the Lord. And this shall be a sign unto you; Ye shall find the babe wrapped in swaddling clothes, lying in a manger. And suddenly there was with the angel a multitude of the heavenly host praising God, and saying,

Glory to God in the highest, and on earth peace, good will toward men."

Verity's bright hair gleamed in the low light. Her intent profile was visible against the glow of the lamp near Dace. Matt watched as she motioned all the girls to stand behind Dacian. They nodded, and the one who'd shouted loudest dragged the lone white girl with her, leading the rest of the girls to the front.

Matt was struck by the simple beauty of the setting. The white candle in each window and on the Christmas tree. The bright faces of the children all sporting the ridiculous head cloths or ribbons. The way the parents leaned forward watching their children. A feeling he couldn't name filled him up.

Dacian's voice quavered with amusement, and then he went on in a serious tone.

"And it came to pass, as the angels were gone away from them into heaven, the shepherds said one to another, Let us now go even unto Bethlehem, and see this thing which is come to pass, which the Lord hath made known unto us."

The five shepherds picked up their canes and walked toward Beth and Alec.

"And they came with haste, and found Mary, and Joseph, and the babe lying in a manger. And when they had seen it, they made known abroad the saying which was told them concerning this child. And all they that heard it wondered at those things which were told them by the shepherds. But Mary kept all these things, and pondered them in her heart. And the shepherds returned, glorifying and praising God for all the things that they had heard and seen, as it was told unto them."

Then the shepherds walked back up the aisle and, passing Matt, disappeared behind the white curtain.

"Now I will read from the Gospel of Matthew, chapter two," Dacian continued.

"Now when Jesus was born in Bethlehem of Judaea in the days of Herod the king, behold, there came wise men from the east to Jerusalem, Saying, Where is he that is born King of the Jews? for we have seen his star in the east, and are come to worship him."

Verity waved on three boys carrying small boxes in their hands.

And as Matt watched them, it occurred to him that the three of them—Samuel, Dace and himself—had been like these boys until they'd been torn apart by slavery. Now years later, they stood together in the same room, something he'd never expected to live to see. The hope for real togetherness rose in him unbidden. He tried to keep it down, but still it rose.

Then Dace's voice, so reminiscent of Dace's late father, came again in the near darkness, sounding so solemn and reverent.

"When Herod the king had heard these things, he was troubled, and all Jerusalem with him. And when he had gathered all the chief priests and scribes of the people together, he demanded of them where Christ should be born. And they said unto him, In Bethlehem of Judaea: for thus it is written by the prophet, And thou Bethlehem, in the land of Juda, art not the least among the princes of Juda: for out of thee shall come a Governor, that shall rule my people Israel. Then Herod, when he had privily called the wise men, inquired of them diligently what time the star appeared. And he sent them to Bethlehem, and said, Go and search diligently for the young child; and when ye have found him, bring me word again, that I may come and worship him also. When they had heard the king, they departed; and, lo, the star, which they saw in the east, went before them, till it came and stood over where the young child was."

The three kings arrived at the barn and greeted Mary and Joseph with a lot of hand-waving, and then they dropped to their knees before the baby.

"When they saw the star, they rejoiced with exceeding great joy. And when they were come into the house, they saw the young child with Mary his mother, and fell down, and worshipped him: and when they had opened their treasures, they presented unto him gifts; gold and frankincense and myrrh. And being warned of God in a dream that they should not return to Herod, they departed into their own country another way."

The three kings rose and walked back up the aisle to the white curtain, striding regally, not little boys in ragged clothes with torn dish cloths tied on their heads.

Matt watched Verity as she gazed forward. When he had arrived home a few minutes ago, he had immediately looked for her at the house as if he weren't really home until he spoke to her. He'd found Samuel, who had been on his way to the school.

When Samuel had told Matt about Verity's Christmas play with both white and black children, Matt marveled at her audacity. Was there anything this woman wouldn't do?

Then, interrupting Matt's concentration, Samuel tapped him on the shoulder before slipping outside.

Dace finished the story.

"And when they were departed, behold, the angel of the Lord appeareth to Joseph in a dream, saying, Arise, and take the young child and his mother, and flee into Egypt, and be thou there until I bring thee word: for Herod will seek the young child to destroy him. When he arose, he took the young child and his mother by night, and departed into Egypt."

Then Dacian looked up and said, as if he were in St. John's on a Sunday morning reading the epistle, "Here endeth the lesson."

"Come out, children, and take your bows!" Hannah called, hurrying the children out from behind the screen. The whole class of children met at the front, bowing and curtsying to loud applause and whistling from all around the room.

In this enthusiastic clamor, Matt heard Verity's triumph. How did she do it? How did she get whites to bring their children here? True, it was only the children of three white families, but they were here. It had to have been Verity's visit to the Daughters of the Confederacy meeting and the precious box she'd entrusted to them that had made the difference.

Listening for Samuel, Matt looked around and found his cousin looking back at him. The tug of family still plagued Matt. But maybe *plagued* wasn't the right word. Dace had come around a lot. Matt felt as if his heart were being drawn toward his cousin.

What do you remember, Dace, of what happened all those years ago?

Dace cleared his throat and the room fell silent. "Now I'm told the children will entertain us with a Christmas song to end this lovely presentation." He nodded and strode to the rear to stand behind his wife, who was already waiting by the door, evidently ready to depart.

Head cocked to one side, Matt listened carefully for sounds from outside. What was taking Samuel so long?

Grinning, the children paraded up the aisle together and with loud whispered reminders from one of the girls, arranged themselves into a choir. Verity nodded and they began singing:

"Children, go where I send thee
How shall I send thee?
I will send thee one by one
One was the little bitty baby
Wrapped in the swaddling clothes
Lying in a manger
Born, born, born in Bethlehem"

Then over the children's singing came a loud thumping on the roof. Matt folded his arms. He shielded his mouth with his cupped hand so no one could glimpse his broadening smile. The children kept singing, but stared at the ceiling above them. Matt stifled a chuckle. He'd enjoy watching this, watching Verity be taken by surprise. And he'd savor her delight.

Chapter Twelve

When Verity heard the sound of a cow bell clanging, she didn't know what to think. Then the door burst open and Samuel stepped inside, carrying a wooden crate. Verity stared at him. The children stopped singing.

"Children!" Samuel shouted. "What do you think just happened?"

"What?" Annie asked breathlessly, her hands pressed together in front of her chin.

The same anticipation made Verity hold her breath.

"Santa heard you singing and stopped by."

Almost all the children began dancing and jumping with excitement. Even Alec looked excited.

Watching the children's eagerness sped Verity's own pulse. She peered ahead, trying to see what was in the crate.

"And do you know what he said?" Samuel asked.

"What?" the children replied.

"Santa said he couldn't stay, but he said you all deserved something special for such good singing. Now you all line up." Samuel turned toward the door, where Verity noticed Matthew lurking in the shadows. "Mr. Ritter is going to hand out Santa's gifts to each of you good boys and girls."

Verity pressed her hands together.

Matthew looked chagrined, but the children lined up, still bouncing on their toes. He took the box Samuel was pushing toward him and sighed loudly.

Verity studied Matthew's stoic expression. How would he handle this?

"What did Santa bring us, mister?" Thaddeus asked, neck craning to see the contents.

A frown creasing his forehead, Matthew hesitated and then gave in. He stooped and lifted the lid of the crate. "Whoa. Look here. Oranges." He pulled out one and handed it to the first girl in line. Not surprisingly, it was Sassy.

The children all squealed, "Oranges! We never got oranges before!" Sassy yelled.

Verity stood to the side of the classroom, watching Matthew handing out the fruit to each thrilled child. Happiness radiated within her. Samuel slipped to her side. "I thought Matthew should hand out the fruit. He bought it in Richmond for your schoolchildren."

"He did?" Verity was surprised and touched. She

couldn't imagine how much these oranges had cost him in Richmond in December. *Oh, Matthew, how dear of thee.* "How did he find out we were having the play?"

"He didn't know until he arrived at the house tonight and I told him about it. He'd planned for you and Beth to deliver them to your students tomorrow on Christmas. I decided it would be more exciting if they were handed out here, tonight. From Santa, of course." Samuel grinned.

This would be a Christmas to remember for these children born into the privations of the war. And Samuel had done right to urge Matthew to hand out the gifts he brought.

The war had left them all trying to catch up on simple pleasures, the delights of everyday life that had been taken for granted before four years of vast suffering and horrible carnage. Before tonight, Matthew probably hadn't ever had the chance to experience the joy of giving to children. Did anything match the joy of watching children excited over Santa?

"You're still coming for dinner tomorrow with your parents?" she asked Samuel.

"Wouldn't miss it—especially since I'm leaving the next day to find Abby."

Verity touched his arm, worried that he might find only pain and loss. *God, be with this good man.*

"Wonderful play." Samuel gripped her hand briefly and then went to stand by his mother and father.

It didn't take Matthew long to hand out all the fruit. Verity enjoyed watching Matthew's smile broaden until it lit up his whole face. Children were good at that—good at reminding adults of what really mattered in life.

The winter wind rattled the windows, reminding the parents to gather their children and head home. At the door, each thanked her as they left. Dacian came over and wished her a merry Christmas.

Verity offered him her hand and said, "I don't know if you'd be able to, but you and Mrs. Ransford would be very welcome to stop over on Christmas Day."

"And will Samuel be coming, too?" Mrs. Ransford snapped.

"Yes, he will be there with his mother and father," Verity replied, not the least bit surprised that Lirit brought this up again.

"Thank you for the invitation," Dacian said. "We may drop by for a cup of cheer."

"Please do," Matthew said, moving to stand by Verity. His nearness topped off her happy glow. She had to stop herself from claiming his arm.

Dacian looked up at his cousin. "Merry Christmas, Matt."

"Same to you."

Verity heard the emotion that Matthew was trying to hide behind his gruff reply. She inched closer to him. He smelled pleasantly of leather and fresh air, an enticing blend.

Dacian shook Matthew's hand. With lifted nose, Lirit led her husband out. And soon the school was empty except for Verity, Joseph, Beth and Matthew, who'd stayed to sweep up the stray straw. Verity listened as Joseph talked to Matthew, drawing out all he'd learned in Richmond about starting the Union League.

Beth yawned and Verity realized it was time to get her to bed. Then Verity would get to play Santa. Her own parents had shocked some of the other Friends by including Santa in their celebration of Christ's birth. But her father had loved the story of the jolly old elf and had scoffed at the naysayers.

Her father would have heartily approved of the gift Samuel and Matthew had given these children this night. Who could disapprove of such innocent joy?

The house was silent as Verity crept down the creaky stairs to slip Beth's Christmas presents into her stocking on the mantel. When she stepped into the moonlit parlor, with its Christmas tree, she was caught up short. Matthew was there also, putting something into Beth's stocking.

He turned to her and whispered, "I got her some new red hair ribbons."

The wonder that Matthew had thought to buy hair ribbons for her little girl caught Verity around the heart and made it impossible for her to speak. Tears came to her eyes and she turned away.

"What's wrong?" he whispered as he came up behind her. "Shouldn't I have bought ribbons?"

She pressed her hand to her mouth, trying to hide the fact that she was fighting tears. "She'll love the ribbons," Verity whispered.

"You're crying." Matthew laid his hands on her shoulders and turned her toward him. "Why?"

Verity shook her head, unable to put into words how his gift had touched her.

Matt tried to think why his putting ribbons in Beth's stocking should make Verity cry, but came up blank. It was just one of those inexplicable things women did. Then he caught her lavender fragrance and his mind went back to the day they'd cut the two Christmas trees. The memory of her lips went through him like a warm west wind.

Then she did something unexpected. Her hand grazed his cheek and slid into the hair over his right ear. In that exquisite moment he thought he might die of the glory of it. It had been so long since any woman had touched him. He savored the sensation like a starving man letting sugar dissolve on his tongue.

In the moonlight she lifted her fair face to his. For the first time he saw the invitation he hadn't known he was waiting for until this moment. Slowly, as if they were puppets on strings, their faces drew toward one another. Their lips met and it was a tender meeting.

Matt closed his eyes and leaned into the kiss. Warmth flooded him. He had yearned for this moment—without even realizing it.

He let his lips roam over hers. They were sweeter and softer than he'd remembered. His thumbs made circles on the collar of her cotton flannel wrapper. Her underlying softness worked on him, melting his final resistance to this woman.

At last he drew back, his hand cupping the back of her head. He looked down into her caramel-brown eyes glistening in the low light. "We're colleagues here and now. But we won't be forever."

She nodded.

Did that mean she agreed that they might be more than colleagues sometime in the future? He couldn't go on without revealing more of his tangled, unexamined feelings than he was prepared for at this time. But this woman had brought healing to Fiddlers Grove—and at least some measure to him.

Because of her, he was speaking to his cousin and had even worked with him to deal with Orrin. He'd thought he'd come here because of his mother's deathbed request. But he had come here to fill in the hole that being forced to leave his home in 1852 had left in his life. He'd come to find his family, his friend Samuel.

And did he indeed love this woman? Was she the right one? *She must be. I've never felt this way about any woman before.*

"Good night," he whispered, making himself end their sweet interlude. Hesitating, hating to leave her, he traced her soft lips with his index finger once and then turned and left.

Verity stood still for a very long time after he'd closed the back door. Then she went and tucked into Beth's stocking the new red mittens and scarf she'd secretly knitted, and a peppermint stick. Verity had already received her own Christmas gift—Matthew's kiss and half-spoken promise.

They had come to an agreement tonight. Both of them were committed to their work here, and that took precedence over their personal feelings. If they went forward as a couple now, she would not be able to focus on her mission as teacher and peacemaker here in Fiddlers Grove. The Freedman's Bureau did not employ married women as teachers.

But if she'd understood Matthew right, a time was coming when she could put widow's black behind her. She leaned her head against the smooth wooden mantel and let lush wonder flow through her every nerve. *Thank Thee, Father, for this very special Christmas gift.*

In the thin wintry sunlight of early January, Verity walked up and down the rows of desks, her skirts swishing over the wooden floor. Friendly voices hummed in the room. Children were quizzing each other, preparing for a spelling test that would start in just a few moments. Then the school door opened and Annie's grandmother burst inside, ushering cold wind into the warm schoolroom.

Matt stared out the kitchen window toward the school through the windbreak of leafless poplars. He wondered how the latest news from Washington would affect their work here. The Richmond newspaper lay on the table. He'd read the headline countless times in the past few minutes. Every newspaper had brought troubling news from Washington, D.C., but this was the worst. It couldn't bode well for them.

President Johnson had been fighting the Radical Republicans in Congress over the South's refusal to ratify the Fourteenth Amendment, which would make former male slaves voting citizens. When Matt thought how the latest development in this conflict might affect the tenuous peace here, his stomach churned. He knew Verity, who'd always had higher hopes than he had, would be devastated.

Matt saw Dace galloping up to the back door. He knocked and entered without invitation. Then Dace pulled the same Richmond paper from inside his coat and shook it at Matt. "Have you seen this?"

Startled, Verity looked up at the woman. "What is it? What's happened?"

"We've found Jesse!"

For a moment Verity could not figure out who Jesse was. And then it came back to her. The day she'd visited the Daughters of the Confederacy meeting, Jesse had been the first lost soldier she'd revealed to the ladies. "Thee did!" Verity shouted in joy.

"Yes." Annie's grandmother swept up the center aisle. She held out a letter in both gloved hands. "I just received a letter from his wife, Louisa. We had contacted the South Carolina militia adjutant and he fowarded our request to the family of the man he believed to be our Jesse. She begs us to send his effects to her."

Thinking of Louisa and the comfort that word of her late husband would give her, Verity could not stop her tears. "Oh, I am so happy, and my sisters will be, too. Oh, praise God." Verity opened her arms and the two women embraced.

Dace halted in front of Matt and looked at the paper on the table. Dace threw his copy on top of Matt's. "You've read it, then?"

"Yes." Matt glanced down again at the headline: Congress Divides South into Five Military Districts.

"It's monstrous," Dace exclaimed. "According to this, Virginia isn't even a sovereign commonwealth anymore. The Union military will rule us. Are you Yankees trying to get us to secede again?"

You Yankees. He and Dace were enemies again. The past few weeks had just been a lull in the long war. Matt rubbed his taut forehead, his gut tightening.

"When my slaves were freed, I lost most of my wealth. Then after the surrender, the Union government confiscated my harvested tobacco and cotton. I'd stored four years of harvests on *my* land that I hadn't been able to sell due to the Union blockade. Then they stole everything but the house, leaving me nearly penniless.

"Now, because before the war I owned too much land to suit the abolitionists in Congress, I was barred from taking the oath of loyalty to the U.S. or holding office. Virginia was in the process of writing a new state constitution. I had hopes of at least regaining the vote. Now this." Dace looked at the paper with loathing.

Dace felt that his right to vote was more important than Samuel's? Matt's ire fired up. "What did you think was going to happen, Dace? The war supposedly settled once and for all the issue of slavery—"

"I can accept the end of slavery," Dace cut in. "I must."

"But you don't accept that Samuel is free now and will vote just like any other man," Matt said. "And people like Orrin Dyke are still actively fighting the changes that freeing the slaves must bring. In other Southern states there have been race riots and lynchings. The slaves can be free as long as they don't act free. Isn't that what you mean, Dace?"

With his clenched fist, Dace hit the table, turned and stalked out.

Annie's grandmother had left to spread the good news. Now Verity stood in front of the row of first-graders and began dictating their spelling words. The children had their chalks poised over their slates and were listening so hard that it made her smile. "Spell *rob.*" Squeaky chalk scribbled on the slates.

The joy of locating the first family of a lost soldier still bubbled inside her. Verity couldn't wait to write her sisters this evening. This was cause for celebration. *Wait until Matthew hears. Maybe now he will believe in the power of love to reach hearts and change minds.* Then she made herself concentrate on the spelling test. "Spell *mob,*" she said.

After school on that happy day, Verity strolled home, lighthearted, through the early twilight. She'd stayed late, tidying up the schoolroom and correcting papers written by the older students. As she approached her home, she noted that there was a strange carriage parked in front of her house. Who could be visiting? Verity hurried up her back steps and into the warm kitchen, where Hannah was standing at the stove. Verity bent to pat Barney as he greeted her. The room was fragrant with the scent of ham roasting. Beth was at the table, doing her homework.

Hannah swung around to face Verity. "I'm glad you come home, Miss Verity," Hannah whispered. "Joseph and Matthew are in the parlor, entertaining two gentlemen. I didn't like the look of them."

Verity took off her gloves, cape and bonnet and hung them on a peg by the door, smoothing back her hair. "Who are they?"

"I don't remember their names, but one is black and one's skinny and white. Looks like he never had a square meal."

Verity grinned. "Do we have enough to invite them to eat supper with us?" Hannah nodded. "Then I'd best go in." Patting Beth on the back, Verity headed to the parlor. She paused at the entrance to the room, a smile of welcome on her face.

Joseph jumped up from his chair, but Matthew made the introductions. "Verity, these two gentlemen, Mr. Alfred Wolford and Mr. Jeremiah Cates, are from the Freedman's Bureau. Gentlemen, this is Mrs. Verity Hardy."

She walked forward, holding out her hand.

The two men who'd stood up were staring at her in a funny way. It turned out that Mr. Wolford was the tall, thin white man and Jeremiah Cates was the large, robust-looking black man. After they had shaken hands, she said, "Please be seated again,

Friends. I'm so happy to entertain thee in my home."

"Don't you mean the Freedman's Bureau's home, young woman?" Mr. Wolford glowered at her.

This caught Verity just as she was about to lower herself into one of the chairs. "I beg thy pardon?"

"This home, in fact, belongs to the Freedman's Bureau, doesn't it?" Mr. Wolford insisted in a scratchy voice that was higher than expected. His Adam's apple bobbed in his scrawny throat.

"Thee knows that is true." Verity sat down. "But why does thee bring it up?"

"We bring it up," Mr. Cates said in his full deep voice, "because rumor has it that you have over-stepped your bounds, ma'am." He sat down again, while Mr. Wolford remained standing.

"Indeed?" She widened her eyes in surprise. "And thee listens to rumors? I never do." Of course she shouldn't have included those final three words. *But it's the truth.*

She glanced at Matthew to see if he could offer her any enlightenment as to what was going on here. He merely stared at her in stony silence. Smothering fear pressed on her lungs. *What do these men want?*

From his stance at the fireplace, Mr. Wolford glared at her. "Young woman, we've heard rumors that the Freedman's school here has openly included white children. And your father-in-law has admitted that this is true." Mr. Wolford sounded as disgruntled as if he were at table and someone had pulled away his plate of food.

"So, ma'am, you see it's good we listen to rumors," Mr. Cates said with a sly, smooth smile.

Her gaze on Matthew, Verity replied, "That is true. We have four white students attending here." As she thought of this triumph, sparkling happiness filled her as usual. "Why shouldn't white children attend public school? They would in the North." Matthew's face was clenched and rigid.

"Now, ma'am, is it fair for children whose parents owned slaves and fought against the Union to receive a free education at the government's expense?" Mr. Cates asked in his rolling baritone. "You are forgetting who the enemy is."

Verity tried to stifle her increasing apprehension, a stiffening at the back of her neck. "Do we still have enemies a year after the war ended? The war is over, Friends. I didn't come here to prolong it. I came to do what President Lincoln wanted us to do. I wanted to bind up the nation's wounds, to bring help and healing here. White children should not be punished for the actions of their parents. And I would think that having white children and black children attending the local school together would advance this—"

"Young woman, this isn't a Christian mission," Mr. Wolford snapped. "The Freedman's Bureau is a government body with very specific purposes paid for by taxes."

She again looked to Matthew, appealing for his backing. He said nothing, but looked back at her with a pained expression. She tried reason again, saying, "I don't understand why four white children in school is objectionable. I assure thee that the black children don't complain. Perhaps thee doesn't understand the situation Mr. Ritter and I faced when we arrived here."

"Mr. Ritter gave us some indication of this, ma'am. But we would be glad to hear what you have to say." Mr. Cates motioned to her to speak.

Some indication? An odd sensation came over her, like ants crawling up her spine. What had Matthew told these men about her? "When we came to Fiddlers Grove, the white people here were set against having a Freedman's school in their town," Verity began.

"And they didn't hesitate to make this known." Joseph spoke for the first time. "They attacked Matt, attacked my daughter-in-law, burned our barn and tried to burn our house down. Or should I say the *Freedman's Bureau's* house down?" Joseph looked flushed and angry. "Why wasn't the Bureau here then to try to protect *its* house and my daughter-in-law?"

Seeing the men's expressions hardening into anger, Verity spoke up, her words stumbling over each other in her haste. "I think that my father-in-law is trying to tell thee that we had a very difficult time at first. But with God's favor, I won some of the people over by appealing to their better selves."

"Young woman, where in your instructions did it say anything about including white children in a Freedman's school?" Mr. Wolford demanded, ignoring what she'd said. "A Freedman's school is to educate black children and adult Negroes—freed slaves—who must learn how to read and write in order to become informed voting citizens."

"Aren't white children supposed to become informed voting citizens, too?" Verity asked in what she hoped was a reasonable tone, fire beginning to burn in her stomach.

"That is not the point in question," Mr. Cates replied, rising to stare down at her. "Are you aware that the former Southern states have been dissolved and the South is now under military jurisdiction? The South is unregenerate. They will not ratify the Fourteenth Amendment, giving former slaves citizenship."

Each word hit her like a well-aimed missile.

"The Freedman's Bureau is a bureau in the War Department," Mr. Wolford added. "You and Mr. Ritter were given very generous funds in order to carry out a specific program to benefit black children and freed slaves, just as Mr. Cates has said. Not to open a school for all the children of Fiddlers Grove, Virginia."

Mr. Cates nodded his agreement.

Verity stared at them in dawning disbelief. *No, no,*

please, no. Were they listening to themselves? "White children sitting in the same building as black children costs the U.S. nothing."

Frowning, Mr. Cates said, "I don't like repeating myself, but you have overstepped your bounds, ma'am. No doubt from the best of motives. But as usual, a woman doesn't easily grasp legal distinctions."

The man's casual insult of her intelligence just because she was female left Verity openmouthed, gasping, speechless. *When someone deems thee inferior because of thy dark skin, does thee like it?* She bit her lower lip to stop herself from tossing this question into his condescending face.

Mr. Wolford moved toward the parlor door. "Mr. Cates and I will be staying in the area. We expect that you will dismiss the white children from the school. Otherwise we will have to inform the Bureau that *you* should be dismissed."

One last time, Verity tried to catch Matthew's eye, but he wouldn't meet her gaze. Her face burned from their scorn.

"Mr. Ritter, we'd like to meet the men you mentioned earlier, the ones you think will carry on the Union League after you leave Fiddlers Grove." Mr. Cates's rich voice boomed in the strained silence in the room.

Matthew was leaving Fiddlers Grove? Verity felt as if she'd been hit with a second hammer.

"Good evening, ma'am." Mr. Cates gave a perfunctory bow and left, followed by Mr. Wolford who gave her only a parting glare. Matthew departed without even a backward glance.

When Joseph returned from seeing the men to the door, he and Verity just looked at one another.

"Does that mean they are going to put Alec and Annie and the other white students out of our school?" Beth stood in the doorway into the parlor, Barney whining at her feet.

Seeing Beth's troubled expression made Verity feel nauseated. She sat back down. "I can't believe… I just can't believe it."

Beth hurried to her, her dark braids bouncing. "You're not going to let them do that to Alec, are you, Mama?"

Verity rested her head on her hand. She tried to understand why Matthew had remained silent while these two bureaucrats had scolded her for doing what God had sent her here to do. Surely there was something she and Matthew could do to avert this. Sending Alec and Annie and the other white children away was too awful to imagine. There must be a way to stop these men from ruining everything.

Then an awful realization trickled through her like icy water. Why did she think Matthew would help her?

Matthew had sat here in the same room and had said nothing to defend her. He'd remained as remote as a disapproving stranger. But then, Matthew didn't support what she'd done here. He'd only tolerated it. At this thought, she pressed a hand to her pained heart. How did that mesh with the promise she thought he'd made to her in this very room on Christmas Eve?

Matthew stepped inside the back door and hung up his jacket and muffler. In the warm, shadowy kitchen, he turned and saw Verity, obviously upset. He'd almost gone to his cabin for the night—he hadn't wanted to face this. But he wasn't a coward. He'd seen the light in the kitchen window and knew that she was up and worried.

I can't do anything about Wolford and Cates. I can't change anything here for her. He felt like a failure. Was this how his father had felt all those years ago when he'd done right but was helpless to change Virginia or to protect his family from injustice?

Verity stared up at him, hurt visible in her warm brown eyes. He folded his arms across his chest to keep from reaching for her.

He searched for something to say, something to keep from discussing what she would want to discuss. What he could do nothing about. What he was helpless to alter. "Hannah's gone home for the night?"

Verity looked confused. "Of course. Did thee eat?"

Food? Had he eaten? "No." His stomach growled as if upon command. He looked past Verity, not wanting to meet her gaze. Facing enemy fire had been less taxing than remaining silent while Cates and

Wolford had berated her. But how could he disagree with them? Everything they'd said was absolutely, point-by-point true.

"Hannah left thee a plate in the warming oven." Verity went to the stove and with the quilted potholders drew out a plate covered with a pie tin. "Will thee sit, please?"

He moved to the dry sink first and washed his hands, wiped them over his face, washing away the dust of the day. He felt as if he'd lived a hundred years since morning. *First Dace and then Wolford and Cates—what a great day.*

When Matt turned, Verity was pouring him a steaming cup of coffee. He sat down at the table and stared at the plate of ham, turnips, biscuits and gravy. Why was she still doing this for him? Didn't she hate him for his unavoidable silence?

She sat across from him and clasped her hands in her lap, leaning forward. "I have some good news."

Watching her try to smile for him sliced him to the quick. "Oh?"

"Yes. Annie's grandmother heard from the family of the first of the lost soldiers. That's good news, isn't it?"

Even this didn't lift his mood. He picked up his fork and began trying to eat, though he had no appetite. He stared at her, mute. *I have no good news for you, Verity.*

"Where has thee been, Matthew?" She betrayed

her nervousness by starting to pleat the red-and-white-checked tablecloth.

He closed his eyes. The weight of powerlessness was nearly crushing the breath from him. After four years of blood and horror, the active war had ended, replaced by a guerrilla war of hard-eyed resistance. That's what Cates and Wolford were fighting.

He'd tried to hold back the sadness that had begun earlier when he'd spoken with Dace. Despair from their brief, harsh exchange had washed over him in wave after relentless wave. They were set on opposite sides just as they had been since the day the good people of Fiddlers Grove had thrown rocks through the windows of his parents' house. In his mind, he heard again the shattering glass, flying, crashing.

"Matthew," Verity said, touching his sleeve, "those two men said I must not let the white children come to school. But I don't know how to do that. If I send the white children away, it will be a betrayal of everything I believe to be right and just."

Her words didn't surprise him. He chewed mechanically. She wasn't the kind of woman to give up, even if peace were something she could never achieve in Virginia. He looked past her, out the dark window.

She tilted her head so she could keep eye contact with him. "In the letter of the law, Mr. Wolford and Mr. Cates are probably right. I was sent here to educate freed slaves and their children. But what happened here was different and special. All over the South, there are lynchings, riots, terrible things happening." Her voice became impassioned. "Here in Fiddlers Grove, we have relative calm. And black children and white children are attending the same school, the school thy cousin told me would be burned down. What we have done here is what should be done all over the South. And they want me to end it. I can't do that. I won't."

He swallowed and looked her in the eye. "If you refuse to do what they say, they will fire you. And then they'll dismiss the white children themselves." He heard his words, stark and harsh. *But it's the truth. We can't avoid the truth, Verity.*

She twisted his sleeve. "Can't thee think of anything I can do to stop those two men from doing this?"

His fork stopped in midair. "No. There is nothing you can do. Sometimes problems are too big to do anything about." *You're a grown woman. Didn't you see this coming?*

"How can you say such a thing, Matthew?" she pleaded.

And then the words that he'd held back for years came pouring out. "When I was twelve, the issue of slave states versus free states spilled over into local politics. A free black man had been captured by roaming slave-catchers. And even though there were witnesses who knew he was free, he'd been forced back into slavery in this county. My father was a lawyer and he gathered the evidence, took the local planter who held this free man as a slave to court and the man was set free.

"Two days later, a mob came at night. They were wearing cloth bags with eyeholes over their heads. They broke all the windows in my parents' house, set the barn on fire and shouted death threats." He looked into Verity's eyes, now shining with tears.

"We packed and left the next day." He put down his fork. The old outrage pushed him up out of the chair. He snatched up his things and walked out into the cold night. *Some things just can't be fixed, and this place will never be home again.*

Chapter Thirteen

The next day, Verity answered a polite knock at her back door. There she greeted Elijah and asked him inside. Before she closed the door, she glanced outside toward Matthew's cabin, wondering if he was coming back to the house today. The only sign of life around the cabin was the white trail of smoke from the chimney. Her longing to see Matthew added to the dull ache within her, an emptiness.

With a knowing eye, Hannah had informed Verity when she'd come down that Matt had come in for an early breakfast and gone directly back to his cabin. Verity smarted over the way they'd parted last night. He'd been so closed off to her. *What can I do about this?* The answer came swiftly. *Nothing.*

Elijah hung his hat on the peg by the door. "Hannah told me about the Yankees telling you to send the white children away. I feel very bad about Alec and the others. Those poor children are only pawns."

"And don't Miss Verity look frazzled?" Hannah went to the stove, warmed Verity's cup and poured Elijah and herself coffee. Then the three sat down at the table together and Verity felt the comfort of their friendship. No longer did Hannah feel unnatural sitting down with her. How much longer would she be here with these dear friends?

"I met Mr. Cates and Mr. Wolford last night. Matthew brought them to my cabin," Elijah said, gazing at her with obvious concern. "They want me to take a leadership role in the new Union League here. But I might not be around much longer."

Hannah halted and stared at her husband. Verity lifted both eyebrows in silent question and looked from Elijah to Hannah and back.

"I received a letter this morning after you left, Hannah. Mr. Dacian read it for me. Our Samuel is on his way here with his intended wife, Abby, and her two children," Elijah announced with evident pride, a sudden rise in his voice, a smile lighting up his whole face.

Hannah threw both hands high. "Thank you, Jesus!"

"Samuel found her, then?" Verity asked. Finally, some good news. She smiled, though the persistent hurt dug its claws into her. "I'm so glad."

Hannah rose and the two embraced.

Choking back tears, Elijah continued, "Samuel tracked down the slaver who bought her. And for a price, he told Samuel the name and town of each of the planters who had bought slaves from him that year. Luckily, the man had kept very precise records."

"So that means I'm already a grandma," Hannah exclaimed, beaming as she wiped away tears with her full white apron. "I can't wait to see them. Oh, praise the Lord. He hath done great things!"

Verity pressed her lips together. Seeing such joy made her burden weigh more heavily upon her. *I am happy for Samuel's family. I am, Lord.*

Elijah's smile was broad and full. "We will make plans for a wedding when they get here." He paused. "I'm so sorry you're having difficulties with those two Yankees."

Like a harsh broom, the mention of Cates and Wolford whisked away Verity's gladness for Samuel and his family. She looked down at the tablecloth.

"I know the men are against what you've done here," Elijah said, "but I think that the League will do a lot of good here." He paused and looked troubled. "We've heard rumors that Orrin Dyke is back in town."

Orrin Dyke. Better and better.

"Well, I sometimes had a hard time believin' that you had white children and black children *together* in a school in Fiddlers Grove," Hannah said matter-of-factly, letting herself down on the chair and making it creak.

"It was a miracle." Suddenly sober, Elijah sipped his coffee.

Verity thought of all God had done here in Fiddlers Grove. It should be happening all over the South, instead of the race riots and lynchings. Every awful and cruel thing that Mr. Cates and Mr. Wolford had said was taking place all over the South. They were only reacting to what, in their opinion, had to be stamped out and stopped, not what should be started. She couldn't blame them. Race hate and resentment and murder were devouring the South. Just as the war had. Hate begot violence and violence begot hate and on and on. Verity's neck hurt and she rested her head on her hand.

Hannah spoke up, "You were doing just fine, Miss Verity. You had the school going and the children were learning and things were looking good here. Elijah and I even thought we might stay."

"I hated to leave my little flock, you see," Elijah added.

"But now when Samuel come, we'll leave with him and Abby and the children to go to New York, where he owns a house and land. It seems what's best." Hannah patted Verity's hand.

"I don't blame you," Verity said. And she didn't. How soon would she be asked to leave?

"What are you going to do about the school?" Elijah asked cautiously.

She pressed a hand to her throbbing temple, trying to overcome the helpless worry that not even prayer had shaken. "I don't see my way clear yet. I keep hoping way will open." How many times had she heard her mother say this phrase—*Way will open.* It meant God would open a way for them to accomplish what He wanted.

God could show Verity a way to keep Alec in school—if that was His will. But how could that not be His will? Verity whispered, "Everything was going so well." But God's Spirit didn't stir within her. She looked around at the kitchen she'd used for less than a year and felt just how hard it would be to leave this place. Leave Matthew.

The very next school day what Verity dreaded happened. Mr. Wolford and Mr. Cates entered her school and walked up to her. "It is plain to see that you are not complying with the dictates of the Freedman's Bureau." Mr. Wolford turned and faced the children. "This school is not for you white children. Leave the books and everything on the desks and go home."

The children had fallen silent and were looking at the two men in utter shock. Alec stood up. "Miss Verity, ma'am, what do you want us to do?"

Before Verity could reply, Mr. Wolford spoke up again, "Mrs. Hardy is no longer the teacher here. This is a school for black children only. You white children must leave right now. Put on your wraps and go home."

Alec looked stubborn. "We don't know who you are. And you're not telling us what to do. This is our school."

Mr. Cates started up the aisle toward Alec.

"Alec!" Verity called out in fear. "Please do as these men say."

Mr. Cates stopped and turned back to Verity. "It's too bad that you did not cooperate with us earlier. Your allowing these white children to attend school just let a few Rebs here get the U.S. government to pay for educating their children and they took advantage of it. But they don't want black children to read or write, or black men to have the vote. You may have thought you were doing right, but you weren't."

She clasped her hands together, holding on for the children's sake.

As if not quite believing this was happening, the white children silently rose from their desks, went to the pegs at the rear of the classroom and put on their coats. Alec looked flushed and angry.

Beth rose and stood in the aisle. "Do I have to go too, Mama?"

Verity didn't know what to tell her own child.

Wolford glared at Beth. "Is this child yours, young woman?"

"Yes."

The two men exchanged glances and Wolford began, "The rules are quite—"

"Beth," Verity interrupted him, "go home to Hannah."

"Miss Verity, ma'am," Annie whimpered at the door, "I don't want to leave school. I like school." Beth stood beside Annie, tears trickling down their cheeks.

Verity blinked her eyes, suppressing her own tears. "I'm sorry, children. I'll think of something."

The white children walked out the door and closed it behind them as the black children sat at their desks, stunned. The two men left without another word. Verity stared down at her desk. *I must not upset the children more than they are already.*

"Ma'am," Sassy said, waving her hand, "I didn't want Annie and Beth to go. They nice white girls. I like them."

Verity looked up. "Yes, they are nice girls. And I know they like you, too, Sassy." Verity's voice trembled. "I hope that I'll be able to find a way to make sure that Annie and the other white children can continue learning." Verity rose and took a deep breath.

"This is what happens after a war, children. I hope thee will remember that. The war will never be over until the hearts of men change. And only God can do that."

She recalled how Matthew had looked last night. Something inside him had shut down. She could see the same look now on the faces of the children. She tried to summon up as much strength as she could, smiling at her students. *I couldn't reach him, Lord. What do I do for Matthew, for the children?* "Now let's get back to our lessons. But I hope thee will never forget what war and hatred can do."

Matt jerked awake. He opened his eyes, feeling groggy. Then he heard gunshots in the distance and shouting—jubilant hooting. *The house! The school!* Heart pounding, he scrambled into his trousers and boots. He grabbed his rifle and charged outside into the cold night.

No light shone in the house, but he saw flickering near the school. He ran over the frozen grass. His breath puffed white in the cool night air. Ahead he saw something burning in front of the school at the far side of the property.

He halted behind the windbreak of poplars and tried to make sense of the scene. A crowd of men yelling the Rebel battle cry with glee and shooting their rifles in the air surrounded the school while a cross burned in front of it. Then it all clicked in place. He'd read about the new Ku Klux Klan, Southerners wearing sheets and masks and burning crosses in front of the houses of anyone who opposed them.

And then the significance of the symbol of their hatred hit him. They were perverting the symbol of Christ, mocking His selfless sacrifice. It didn't matter that Matt had felt far from God through the awful bloody war. No one—no one—had the right to show such scorn to Christ.

Flames of outrage roared inside Matt. He champed at the bit to charge forward and extinguish this insult to all that was holy. But he was outnumbered. He stood still, his rifle ready. If anyone moved to torch the school, he'd shoot them where they stood. Minutes passed. He gripped his rifle. Ready to aim. Ready to fire.

Then in the darkness, a horse with two riders galloped close to Matt, heading toward his cabin. Matt was torn, but he recognized one of the riders—Dace. Matt raced after them. *Why would Dace be coming for me?*

As Matt ran after them, the second rider—Samuel—looked back. And then Dace pulled up on his reins. Samuel sat behind him. Matt bounded up to him. "What is it?" Matt asked, breathless.

"The cross burning's just a diversion!" Dace shouted over the gunshots and yelling. "Dyke's attacking your Quaker!" Samuel slid from the saddle and motioned toward Matt. He leaped up behind Dace. He threw his free arm around his cousin, holding his rifle high.

The two of them galloped on toward the house. The commotion around the schoolhouse filled the air with noise. As they approached the house, Matt could see, by the scant moonlight, Orrin on the front porch, striking Verity.

The big man was backhanding and forehanding her. Matt jumped from the saddle. As he ran forward, he caught a flicker of motion to his left. With instincts forged in battle, he turned and squeezed off a shot. An unseen man yelled. And then Matt was charging up the steps.

Matt raised his rifle to aim at Orrin, the sound of Verity's screams sending rage coursing through him. Before he could shout for Orrin to stop, someone collided with him, knocking the rifle from his hand. In the darkness, hands grabbed Matt by the throat, strangling him. "Hey! Orrin! It's the Yankee Ritter! Can I kill him?"

Matt struggled to break the man's grip around his throat.

"No! That Yankee is mine!" Orrin rammed Matt. His meaty fists once again pounded Matt's face, rattling his head. Matt fought back, but Orrin was a bigger man. Matt drew up every bit of his stamina and strength. *Where's Verity? I have to get to my rifle.* Suddenly another gunshot sounded. Orrin jerked and flew backward. Matt staggered. Gasping, he lunged for his rifle. He fell to his knees feeling for his gun.

Another shot. Matt lifted his rifle and rolled to shoot Orrin, but the brute was down.

"Matt!" Dace called from the shadows below the porch. "Are you all right?"

Matt tried to catch his breath, but couldn't.

Then Dace was there helping him to his feet. "Are you shot?"

Matt shook his head. Then he rushed the few steps to Verity. Sweeping her up, he carried her inside the parlor and laid her on the love seat. "Verity? Verity?" He ran his hands lightly over her, feeling for blood soaking her clothing and for limbs twisted in awkward angles. No blood. No broken bones. He gasped with relief.

But she'd fainted. Or had Orrin knocked her unconscious—or worse? He pressed his head against her chest, listening for her heartbeat. It was rapid but strong. He looked around for the rest. "Joseph? Beth?"

"Here. I'm here." Joseph staggered into the room, supported by Dace. "When they broke down the door, they knocked me out." Dace helped Joseph onto the rocker by the fireplace. "Beth's sleeping."

Then Samuel came in, his rifle in hand. "Why don't you build up the fire, Matt? So we can see what needs tending here." Samuel walked over and lit the oil lamp on the mantel. Though he didn't want to leave Verity's side, Matt started a fire in the hearth.

Then Dace and Samuel stood around the love seat where Matt again knelt, all of them gazing down at Verity, unconscious. Her lip had been split and her eye was swollen. Matt wanted to kill Orrin Dyke with his bare hands. Dace handed him a handkerchief and Matt dabbed her lip with it. Rage still tore through him.

He looked up at Dace. "Is Dyke dead?"

"Yes, I shot him," Samuel answered.

Dace glanced at Samuel, shocked.

Matt could feel only satisfaction. The bully would never strike a woman or child again. "Dyke must have set up the cross-burning to cover attacking Verity."

"Probably." Samuel still looked angry and ready to shoot more Klansmen.

"I shot one of his lowlife cousins," Dace said. "Matt, you must have winged another one, who hightailed it away. I'm sorry we didn't get here sooner, but Alec had to run the whole way from his place to mine. He'd overheard what his dad was going to do and he came for me to stop it."

Matt heard the bitterness, anger and irony in his cousin's voice. "You didn't know, then, that the Klan has popped up here?" Matt asked his cousin.

Dace gave him a dark look. "I thought it was just a matter of time. But burning a cross is one thing. Attacking this good lady is quite another. I wouldn't permit *any* woman to be attacked, even if she hadn't saved my life."

Dace's words ignited the flash and flame of Matt's old anger. "Well, at least you did more for this lady and her family than your father did for my family all those years ago. When they broke out all the windows and rode around our house shooting guns, my mother was terrified. She trembled and wept for days."

"At least she survived," Dace snapped. "If my father hadn't stepped in, all three of you would have been lynched that night."

Matt gawked at his cousin.

"I'm not saying it was right. But your father knew the temper of the county at that time—"

"He did what he knew was right," Matt declared, rising. "That man was a free black and he didn't deserve what had been done to him. The judge would have been happy to rule against the man, but the facts and documents were crystal clear." He glanced down at Verity, still lying silent and motionless.

Dace frowned. "I didn't know that. All I know is my father let it be known that if any harm came to your family, he would make the ones involved pay for it with their lives. He was prepared to call out anyone who harmed them."

"Dace." Samuel spoke up in his steady, cool voice. "From your way of thinking that was what your father should have done in the situation. But to my way of thinking, Matt's father shouldn't have been in danger for seeking justice for a black man. Just for doing what was right. If you'd been that free black, how would you have felt being pressed back into slavery?"

The three friends stared at each other.

Samuel continued in that calm, clear voice, "I know what it felt like to be a slave. And the fact that I ran away should have told you what I thought of it."

"Why did you run away?" Dace sounded as if he'd long wondered about this.

A brand-new thought pierced Matt. Had Dace missed him and Samuel? *I never thought of that.*

Samuel sucked in breath. "I fell in love with Abby—you all knew that. But by the time I was fifteen, I realized that I could never protect her. I could marry her but still not keep her safe from any white man who would want her." Samuel's voice was tinged with anger. "Falling in love made me feel powerless in a way I had not before. And I realized that no matter how long I stayed here or how hard I worked, I would never be more than a *boy.* I would never be a man. I couldn't stand that, so I made my plans and my connections and I got on the Underground Railroad, headed north."

"No one would have harmed Abby on our plantation," Dace said, sounding defensive.

"Are you sure about that?" Samuel challenged with keen sarcasm.

"My father and I—"

"What about your overseer, Dace?" Samuel asked. "What about the fact that though Abby's family had been slaves on the Ransford plantation for over a hundred years, your wife sold Abby South—away from her people—just so she could buy a new dress?"

Silence. Matt watched Dace chew the inside of his cheek, an old childhood sign of stress. Dace clearly didn't like what he was hearing, but it was the truth.

"Samuel, your leaving didn't help Abby any." Joseph spoke up, reminding Matt he was in the room.

Samuel looked stung. He gave a dry, mirthless chuckle. "I was only fifteen. I wasn't very wise at that age." He paused. "Dace, slavery is still tearing you all apart. How many people have to die before the South admits it was wrong? Before you admit that my dark skin doesn't make me less of a man?"

Matthew waited for Dace to reply to Samuel's question. But Dace gave no answer. Evidently Dace would not willingly accept a future that included free black men voting. Dace sat down on the love seat and put his head in his hands. "Lirit ran off today. She left me a note and took off with some stranger."

Matt looked at Samuel. This news shocked neither of them. Matt leaned over to listen to Verity's heart-beat again. Her soft hair tickled his face. *Please wake up. Soon.*

"You're well rid of that woman." Joseph spoke up. "Find yourself a sweet woman this time. Pretty lasts only so long. True beauty that shines from a woman's heart lasts for eternity. And it helps if she's a good cook." Joseph smiled and then rose from the rocker. "Will one of you help me up to my bed? I'm an old man and I'm feeling it tonight. Thank God little Beth slept through all this. The sleep of the innocent."

Samuel went to help Joseph. Dace said, "I'll go get

help to remove Orrin and his cousin's bodies. And I'll put out the word that I killed them."

Matt knew why Dace was telling this lie—it was to protect Samuel and his family. Otherwise, the Klan would come after them.

Samuel paused at the door and looked back at Dace. "Thank you, Dace. And how would you like to host my wedding to Abby in a couple of days?"

"I'd like that fine," Dace said, then exhaled deeply. "I'd like to see you and Abby happy. And you, too, Matt. If you let Mrs. Hardy slip through your fingers, you're a blockhead."

Matt felt a soft hand squeeze his and looked down. "Verity." He took her hand and kissed it.

"Matthew," she whispered, her eyes worried. "Where—"

"I'm here. Don't be frightened. Orrin's gone and we're all safe." He gently stroked the hair that had come loose from her hairpins. The past now made some sort of sense.

Dace, just like his father, had been caught up in the blindness of slavery but had not abandoned Matt's parents then. Or Matt now. Now he knew why Samuel had run away. And now Samuel had found Abby and was going to marry her. Even Dace had been given a second chance. He was well rid of Lirit. Matt heard his cousin's words again: *If you let Mrs. Hardy slip through your fingers, you're a blockhead.*

Verity whispered, "I was frightened. Beth, is she—"

"Beth slept through it all somehow. Don't worry." He kissed her forehead without thinking.

"Matthew, thee is kissing me again. What does that mean?"

"It means you're going to marry me, Verity Hardy. As soon as Cates and Wolford get another teacher here, you'll quit teaching. I'm going to take good care of you and Beth. And nothing is ever going to separate us again."

Verity drew in a deep breath. "Yes. Nothing is going to separate us again. But, Matthew, the children—"

He bent down and kissed her bruised lips gently. *She will be mine and I will be hers.* Then he swept her up and carried her toward the stairs. "I'll put you to bed, but I'm sleeping here in the parlor. I'm not taking any chances with your safety tonight."

"Whatever thee thinks is best, Matthew."

Matt grinned. He wondered how often his headstrong wife would repeat those words in the years to come. The corners of his mouth tried to crinkle up. *Thank you, Father, for this woman. I probably don't deserve her, but I'll do my best for her and Beth. With Thy help.*

Three days later Matt, Verity, Joseph and Beth, with Barney jogging happily by their side, walked to the Ransford plantation. A January thaw had blown in the day before. Today was balmy, sunny with beautiful white clouds floating in a true blue sky. When they reached the manor, they saw a large crowd of former slaves gathered on the sunny south lawn, dressed festively. Many happy voices were already singing. Matt led his family to join them. His family. A feeling of joy expanded inside him as he pondered those words.

As they approached the group, Matt was somewhat surprised to see Pastor Savage there. In the past Dacian Ransford, and his father before him, had performed slave marriages. But of course Samuel and Abby were not slaves anymore. Matt easily recognized Abby, whom he had not seen since he left in 1852. She was a very handsome young woman, despite the harsh blows life had dealt her. A boy who looked a bit older than Beth stood on one side of her and a little girl on the other side. During the marriage ceremony, the boy shyly moved to stand beside Samuel, and Samuel took his hand.

Matt felt good seeing Samuel, Abby, her children, and Hannah and Elijah so happy. The outdoor wedding proceeded, with solemn ceremony. Hannah and Elijah stayed at the front of the gathering, beaming.

Matt looked at Verity, who still showed signs of Orrin's attack. She had one blackened eye and a bruised face, and she moved slowly. He thought she might have a cracked rib. Would he ever forget seeing her struggling with Orrin? *No one will ever hurt her again,* he swore to himself. *No one.*

Gritting his teeth, Matt dragged his focus back to Samuel and Abby in time to hear Pastor Savage announce, "I now pronounce you man and wife. I present to you all today Mr. and Mrs. Samuel Freeman."

The gathering shouted and clapped with approval. Beth stood up and cheered. "Samuel got married, Mama!"

Verity smiled and nodded. Then her eyes met Matt's. She blushed and he smiled, tucking her closer. They would tell Beth tonight of their intentions to wed.

Before long, the gathering was dancing and singing. Samuel drew Abby's arm through his and led her and her two children toward Matt.

"Mr. Matt," Abby greeted him. "I'm happy to see you again. And this is your lady?"

"Yes," he said, drawing Verity's hand over his arm and wrapping his other arm around Beth.

Verity smiled. "Who are these lovely children?"

"This is my son, Ezra, and my daughter, Delia. Make your bows, children," Abby said. Both children obeyed, grinning shyly.

"How soon is thee taking thy family to Albany, Samuel?" Verity asked.

"We will be leaving tomorrow," Samuel said. "My father and my mother will be traveling to New York with us by train. I own a house near Albany with six acres."

Verity squeezed Matt's hand in hers. "We will miss

thee. But perhaps after Matthew finishes his work for the Freedman's Bureau, we can visit thee."

"Both Abby and I would like that." Samuel stroked Delia's tightly braided hair and put a hand on Ezra's shoulder.

Matt drew in the hint of lavender that would always mean Verity to him. He wished she wouldn't wear that bonnet. Perhaps after they were married, he would suggest she stop wearing it so he could see her lovely face. He smiled at the thought of her reaction to this suggestion.

Beth was wearing the red ribbons Matthew had given her for Christmas. She glanced up at him and smiled, her innocent affection cutting through any remnant of his hard soldier's heart.

Dace approached them with Alec. "May I wish you every joy, Samuel and Abby."

Abby curtsied and looked down.

"Thanks, Dace." Samuel held out his hand. "And thanks for allowing us to hold our wedding here."

Dace hesitated and then gripped Samuel's hand. "Don't mention it."

Alec moved to Verity's side. "I'm going to miss coming to school, ma'am," he said.

Matt was pleased to see the boy here. Orrin had been buried and mourned by very few, least of all by his wife and son. Orrin had been given a sweet wife and a good son and he'd treated them like trash. Why?

Verity patted Alec's shoulder. "It will only be for a little while."

"What do you mean?" Alec asked, hope in his voice.

"After I'm replaced at the Freedman's school, I'm going to invite any child who wishes to learn to come to my house every morning at eight. I can hold school around the kitchen table."

Shaking his head, Matt gently pulled Verity closer. "And when, dearest, were you going to tell me about this plan?" he asked, trying to suppress a grin.

Verity chuckled. "About now."

Matt let out a joyous, boisterous laugh. Life would be good with Verity and his new family by his side. He was finally home.

Epilogue

Verity sat in the kitchen in Fiddlers Grove, holding a letter. She'd written her family about her coming marriage to Matthew, and her sister Felicity had written right back.

Dearest Verity,

I'm so happy to hear about thy finding someone to love again. Matthew must be a very special man. Mercy and I still plan to remain spinsters. But we will take the train to Richmond and then hire a wagon to drive to Fiddlers Grove. We wouldn't miss thy wedding.

I have news, too. Does thee remember my friend Mildred? She passed away a month ago in Illinois. And I never expected it, but she has left me a bequest—her house! I had been praying for a way to help all the orphans left by the terrible war. Now I will be able to start a home for them! And the location couldn't be better, since her town is right on the Illinois side of the Mississippi River just north of St. Louis. It will make it so much easier for orphans to reach us. I am so excited.

We will see thee soon.

Love,

Felicity

* * * * *

Mark your calendars so you don't miss Felicity's story next December 2009!
Three Christmas stories for three special sisters—
Verity, Felicity and Mercy.

Dear Reader,

I hope you have enjoyed reading about Verity Hardy and her crusade after the Civil War. In 1861, the disagreement between the free and slave states about the westward spread of slavery finally broke into open war. After bloodshed, it took nearly a century before the North and South began to draw back together. In our own lives, we must guard against causing such deep breaches with our loved ones. We must never say harsh words that might not be forgotten or do anything that would take years to forgive. And we must ask God to help us forgive and forget when we are wronged.

Verity was right. The Freedman's Bureau should have followed her example of reconciliation that comes from true forgiveness. Forgiving someone doesn't say that no wrong has been done. Forgiveness merely releases the unforgiving heart from bondage. "Blessed are the peacemakers for they shall be called the children of God."

Lyn Cote

QUESTIONS FOR DISCUSSION

1. If someone you love was planning to go into a dangerous situation because she thought God was leading her there, what would you say to her?

2. Do you think it was right for Verity to take her young daughter along with her into such a dangerous situation? Why or why not?

3. How could a good man fight for slavery? Why did Dacian Ransford and Robert E. Lee choose Virginia over the Union?

4. Could the North have done something differently after the Civil War in order to prevent what happened to former slaves after the Radical Republicans no longer controlled Congress?

5. How did Verity begin to change the negative attitude in Fiddlers Grove?

6. Why was Verity's work of charity so important to her?

7. Compare and contrast Samuel, Matt and Dace. What made them friends when they were children?

8. Do you agree with Samuel's reasons for running away? Why or why not?

9. Have you seen or read *Gone with the Wind* by Margaret Mitchell? If so, do you think Hannah and Elijah would accept the portrayal of the slaves after emancipation in that watershed novel? Why or why not?

10. What did you learn about this historical period that you hadn't known before?

11. Look up *verity* in the dictionary. Do you think this is an appropriate name for the heroine of this book? Why or why not?

12. Do you think there was any way to avoid the Civil War?

13. If you'd lived during the Civil War, how would you have argued with anyone who justified slavery by pointing to references in the Bible?

14. Why do you think the South could not accept the end of slavery and the equality of black people?

REQUEST YOUR FREE BOOKS!

2 FREE INSPIRATIONAL NOVELS
PLUS 2
FREE
MYSTERY GIFTS

Love Inspired
HISTORICAL
INSPIRATIONAL HISTORICAL ROMANCE

YES! Please send me 2 FREE Love Inspired® Historical novels and my 2 FREE mystery gifts (gifts are worth about $10). After receiving them, if I don't wish to receive any more books, I can return the shipping statement marked "cancel". If I don't cancel, I will receive 4 brand-new novels every other month and be billed just $4.24 per book in the U.S. or $4.74 per book in Canada, plus 25¢ shipping and handling per book and applicable taxes, if any*. That's a savings of over 20% off the cover price! I understand that accepting the 2 free books and gifts places me under no obligation to buy anything. I can always return a shipment and cancel at any time. Even if I never buy another book, the two free books and gifts are mine to keep forever. 102 IDN ERYA 302 IDN ERYM

Name	(PLEASE PRINT)	
Address		Apt. #
City	State/Prov.	Zip/Postal Code

Signature (if under 18, a parent or guardian must sign)

Mail to Steeple Hill Reader Service:

IN U.S.A.: P.O. Box 1867, Buffalo, NY 14240-1867
IN CANADA: P.O. Box 609, Fort Erie, Ontario L2A 5X3

Not valid to current subscribers of Love Inspired Historical books.

Want to try two free books from another series?
Call 1-800-873-8635 or visit www.morefreebooks.com

LIH08R

Luke Harris grew up
without a family, and now
that's all he wants. Even
more so when he moves
next door to widowed
mom Janie Corbett and
her three kids. For the
first time, he can imagine
having a wife and children
to call his own. But the
once-burned-twice-shy
Janie won't accept Luke's
attentions...until he
confronts his troubled past.

Look for

A Family for Luke
by
Carolyne Aarsen

*Available January
wherever books are sold.*

Steeple
Hill®

www.SteepleHill.com

LI87512

Love Inspired.

HISTORICAL

TITLES AVAILABLE NEXT MONTH

Don't miss these two stories in January

SECOND CHANCE BRIDE by Jane Myers Perrine
On the run from a shameful past, Annie MacAllister plans
to act as the new schoolteacher in Trail's End. At least until
she's saved up enough money to start her life over. Soon
Annie catches the eye of John Sullivan, upstanding citizen,
the father of one of her students and a man capable of
exposing her troubled past. Together they will need
some divine forgiveness to rekindle their faith and find a
future together.

THE PATH TO HER HEART by Linda Ford
Widowed father Boothe Wallace has a hard time trusting
the medical profession, which he blames for his greatest
loss. Until he meets sweet, beautiful nurse Emma Spencer.
Emma's own secret pain leads her to think her dreams of a
family will never come true. But when Boothe asks her to
play his temporary fiancée to protect his son, she knows
God can see exactly what her heart is yearning for....

LIHCNM1208BPA